'Lucy broke into a run, willing the strength back into her wobbly legs. She didn't know if the man had started to run too. She could hear nothing but her own heart banging madly in her ears. As she neared the corner she put on a tremendous spurt, then ran diagonally across the side street and through the gateway of a semi-detached house, whose small front lawn was bounded by a six-foot-high privet hedge.

She cowered behind the dripping hedge, shaking and gasping, praying that no one in the house would look out of a front window and see her. Her luck held. No one spotted her. And a few seconds later she heard feet running past on the pavement. She had been right, then! The bearded man had been after her . . . '

Someone is following fourteen-year-old Lucy Bell. A thin, bearded stranger. What does he want? And who can she turn to for help?

TWISTED TRUTH is Elsie McCutcheon's first novel to be published by Corgi Freeway Books.

TWISTED TRUTH

ELSIE McCUTCHEON

CORGI
FREEWAY

For my friend, Sheila Ferguson

TWISTED TRUTH
A CORGI FREEWAY BOOK 0 552 52592 8

First published in Great Britain by J. M. Dent & Sons Ltd.

PRINTING HISTORY
J. M. Dent edition published 1988
Corgi Freeway edition published 1990

Corgi Freeway Books are published by Transworld Publishers Ltd.,
61-63 Uxbridge Road, Ealing, London W5 5SA, in Australia by
Transworld Publishers (Australia) Pty. Ltd., 15-23 Helles Avenue,
Moorebank, NSW 2170, and in New Zealand by Transworld Publishers (N.Z.) Ltd., Cnr. Moselle and Waipareira Avenues, Henderson, Auckland.

This book is set in 11/12 Palatino by
Chippendale Type, Otley, West Yorkshire

Printed and bound in Great Britain by
Cox & Wyman Ltd, Reading

Contents

1

Missing Person

It was her mother and David talking in the living-room that had wakened Lucy. She was glad they had. Normally she slept late on Saturday mornings. But today she was going into town with Fiona Donald to help her choose new shoes. She didn't know what time it was, because she had mislaid her watch. But, she thought, hearing her four-year-old brother, Reuben, playing in the back garden, it must be after nine o'clock.

'B-room b-room b-room,' went Reuben negotiating a nasty corner at Brands Hatch. 'Here, you! Wee yin! Belt up an' give us some peace!' someone bawled angrily. It was old Hamish Henderson who lived upstairs at number eight.

And if the McIvers who lived at number six hadn't been away in Torremolinos, they would have been shouting at Reuben too, Lucy thought uncomfortably.

'B-room b-room,' went Reuben, paying no attention to Hamish.

Lucy sat up in bed, her cheeks hot with embarrassment. Mum and David must have heard Hamish. Why didn't they stop Reuben making that noise? Why was she the only one in the family who cared what other people thought? It was always the same. What had happened last year, after all, when they had moved here to Old Whitefields? Lucy had fully expected her mother to introduce herself to her new neighbours as 'Mrs Darcy'. But not a bit of it! It had been 'Mrs Bell' and 'Mr Darcy' once again. And Lucy had had to explain to her form-tutor in her new school that David Darcy was not her legal stepfather. She had hated doing that. There may well have been other kids in the same boat, but Lucy still felt awkward about it. She still imagined the teachers were looking disapproving and the pupils were giggling and nudging one another behind her back.

Lucy had tackled her mother about it when she got home after that first day at school. She had asked her straight out why on earth she didn't marry David. To her horror Mum's face had turned the colour of the Cherryade on the sideboard, and her lower lip had begun to tremble. For a moment Lucy had thought she was going to burst into tears. She hadn't, though. She had murmured something about a pension and how she would lose it if she married again which wouldn't be sensible. Then she had rushed out into the garden and spent ages unpegging the washing.

Lucy had been puzzled by her mother's explanation. The truth was, she had never thought of Mum as being a particularly sensible person. For a start she dressed really weirdly most of the time in ankle-length skirts and dresses and dark-coloured capes. (Lucy often wondered with a shudder what she was called behind her back in the various schools she visited to teach the violin and piano.)

There was her attitude to paying bills, too.

This really worried Lucy, since David was just as daft in this respect. Mum very often just shoved the bills to the back of the bureau and forgot all about them. Then when the man arrived to cut off the electricity, she would stare at him aghast and cry, 'But surely it's been paid! Months and months ago . . . Oh, no! Don't tell me!' And she would close her eyes and groan, making the Electricity Board man feel really uncomfortable as he went about the disconnecting. After that, until the supply was restored, they would have to use the camping gas cooking-rings and lamps and heaters that were kept in the lobby-cupboard.

The telephone was sometimes cut off as well. And, more than once, Lucy had arrived home from school to find that the television set had been taken back to the rental-shop.

Mum couldn't take money seriously. That was her trouble. And she couldn't understand those people who became fierce and angry about it, like her sister, Rose, and her mother. Gran Campbell – Mum's mother – could not bear untidiness of any sort, and that included people being careless with money. Mum often said that if you stood still for too long in Gran's house, she would come and dust you.

Thinking about Gran Campbell reminded Lucy of her watch. Gran had sent her one for her birthday. If she could find it, she would know what the time really was. (It was a Winnie-the-Pooh watch, not perhaps the ideal gift for a fourteenth birthday, but it had come in handy, since Lucy's own watch had 'walked' out of the gymnasium changing-room last term.)

Lucy rolled over so that her head hung down over the side of the bed. It was a cabin-bed with three drawers and two cupboards in its base. At the moment these were all lying open with their contents spilling out.

She reached down and poked about for a bit among the picture-postcards, old photographs, and notebooks. But there was no sign of her watch. She sat up with a groan. She would have to get out of bed. There was nothing else for it. She had arranged to meet Fiona Donald at the bus terminus at eleven. So she really must find out what time it was.

To get out of bed Lucy had to stick her legs straight out in front of her, then launch herself forward over the open drawers and cupboard doors as though she were leaping over the 'horse' in the gym. The room was so small that she landed on her feet almost at the window. She stepped forward and pulled back the curtains just in time to wave at Reuben as he did a 'no hands' lap of the washing-green.

In fact there wasn't much 'green' to be seen, since most of the grass had been run off by the football-playing boys who had lived in number ten before Lucy and her family moved in. So Old Hamish's washing, and their own, had to dangle over a square either of hard-baked earth, or of squelchy mud, according to the weather. At the moment it was hard earth.

Beneath Lucy's window and the window of the adjoining living-room was her family's part of the back garden. It consisted of a piece of grass with a bench on it, a plot of rhubarb gone wild and a decrepit old garden shed. The rhubarb was useful only to the neighbourhood cats who used it as a hide from which to pounce on the birds that Lucy's mother fed.

Old Hamish had the plot at the foot of the

garden. He drove Mrs McIver wild. When he was tipsy he bawled over the fence to tell her that she ought to go in for conservation like he did. Since he hadn't put a spade near his ground for years, it produced mainly nettles, with the odd poppy for a spot of colour.

The rest of the garden was just grass – long grass, until David got round to cutting it. The strip that ran along the side of the house, past Lucy's family's door, belonged to the upstairs flat. Lucy's family, on the other hand, had the grass square in front of the building, at the foot of the six steps leading up to Old Hamish's door. In Lucy's opinion the town-planner who had thought up the lay-out of Old Whitefields housing-scheme must have been deranged.

Looking around her, Lucy decided her room was reaching one of its periodic peaks of untidiness. The cabin-bed which had been bought last year to help solve this problem seemed only to have made it worse. The clothes which had fitted into her old chest-of-drawers, were too many for the slim drawers in the base of the bed. Little columns of them now sprouted from the floor like multi-coloured stalagmites. She chose a sweater from one, a tee-shirt from another, and gave a helping hand to a pair of knickers that were halfway out of their drawer. Her jeans were straddling an ancient record-player which hadn't worked for years, but which for some reason sat on top of her book-cupboard.

Could her watch have found its way to her dressing-table, she wondered. (Crossing the room was like negotiating an obstacle-course. Just as well it was only eight paces wide!) David had made her the dressing-table three years ago as a project for his evening school do-it-yourself

11

course, so it was very basic. In fact it was only three pieces of white wood nailed together with a spotty mirror sticking up at the back. At the moment it was a disaster-area, she had to admit. Gran Campbell would have been sick on the spot had she seen it.

She chucked two empty Coke cans and a half-eaten Fudgo bar into her rubbish-bin, making a mental note to empty it soon, in case the Fudgo brought the mice back. She picked up some pieces of blue hair as gingerly as though they belonged to someone else, and dropped them on top of the Coke cans. Fiona Donald's sister, Ailsa, who was an apprentice at the 'Cut 'n Colour' hairdressing-salon, had talked Lucy into having red and blue streaks the last time she was practising on her. And Lucy had been trying to get rid of them ever since.

The big bottle of purple lotion that the doctor had given her for her spots was sitting on page 12 of *A Midsummer Night's Dream*. When she lifted it up, it brought half of Oberon's speech with it – the one about 'Cupid's fiery shaft' being 'quench'd in the chaste beams of the watr'y moon'. Lucy had been trying to learn it by heart for Tuesday. She picked the book up and peered at it anxiously. It looked awful! Half the page was totally unreadable. Aggie, who was positively maniacal about books, would be furious. Mr Walton, their regular English teacher, was about to go off on a course, and the Head of English, Mrs McLintock (known throughout the school as 'Aggie') was to take 3A for Shakespeare.

At the beginning of the session Aggie marched into every English class to tell the pupils how no one in Whitefields Comprehensive ever had to share an English book, and how lucky they were

12

compared with the pupils in other schools. Then she went on to give a lecture about how they must now do their part by treating the books like precious objects, and giving them paper covers, and never on any account turning down the corners of pages or breaking the spines.

Lucy looked at what had once been Oberon's speech and felt sick. Aggie mustn't see it. She mustn't! She would go bananas. She would just have to sneak another copy of the *Dream* from the book-cupboard in Aggie's room. Her class was in there on Monday with the student. It shouldn't be too difficult.

Suddenly she noticed a pink strap sticking out from under the Lennon poster that kept falling down from the wall on to her dressing-table. It was her watch. She pulled it out, then stared at it in amazement. According to the black figures on Pooh's yellow tummy, it was eight twenty-three. Eight twenty-three! What on earth were her mother and David doing up at this time on a Saturday morning? And why had Reuben been let out to create merry-hell in the garden? (He was working himself up into a frenzy out there; it sounded more like the outbreak of World War Three than a race at Brands Hatch.)

Lucy crossed to the door, and was just about to open it, when the voice of the man whom she had thought was David said, 'Well, I'll leave you to get dressed and have something to eat, Mrs Bell. I'll be in touch if I hear anything. You'll do likewise, I take it?'

'Yes, yes . . . ' Lucy's mother began. Then her voice faded as she and the man moved out of the living-room into the lobby.

Lucy opened her door quietly, just in time to hear the visitor sigh heavily and say, 'Oh dear! I hate anything like this.' Then the outside door slammed shut, and her mother came back into the living-room.

Mrs Bell was looking down at the floor and shaking her head as though she could not believe what she had heard. To begin with, Lucy thought that she was upset because the visitor had mistaken her Paisley-patterned frock for a nightdress. But as soon as her mother looked up, she realized how stupid she had been. Mum looked nearly demented with worry, her hair wild, and her eyes staring out of a chalk-white face.

'Mum! What's happened?' Lucy cried.

'I don't know,' said her mother tremulously, 'David seems to have disappeared. It's terrible. I can't think what to make of it. That man who has just gone . . . he's David's boss. He hasn't seen David since Wednesday morning. And I haven't seen him since yesterday at breakfast.'

Lucy's heart gave a sickening lurch. She suddenly had a premonition that a terrible calamity was approaching. It was her Celtic intuition at work. She had inherited it from her father, Marmion Bell.

2

Not Lucy's Problem

Lucy washed and dressed as quickly as she could before making her mother a cup of camomile tea. Mrs Bell always drank camomile tea when she was upset. While she was waiting for it, she practised her deep breathing. Hearing her mother's first long intake of breath, Lucy thought she was sobbing and came rushing out of the kitchenette to comfort her. But Mrs Bell waved her away.

'It's all right, pet, I'm just pulling myself together. This is what I used to do before I gave recitals . . . and when I was having babies,' she added as an afterthought.

She certainly looked calmer by the time Lucy handed her the cup of tea. Her eyes were no longer starting out of her head.

Lucy moved the clothes-basket from the piano-stool and sat down, swinging her legs nervously back and forward. 'Do you want to talk about it, Mum?' she asked eventually.

Her mother frowned unhappily. 'I suppose I'll have to,' she said. 'But I want you to understand that this is my problem, Lucy. You're too young to worry about such matters. You mustn't be distracted from your schoolwork.'

She sighed and stared into the fireplace where

15

last night's ashes were creeping out on to the hearth. 'You saw that David didn't come home for tea last night,' she went on after a minute. 'I made nothing of it because I thought he'd been held up at a client's and hadn't had a chance to phone. But after you went to bed I began to get worried. I waited until eleven and then I phoned David's boss, Mr Tomney – the man who's just left. He told me David hadn't been into the office for two days – not since Wednesday morning. Mr Tomney had arranged a meeting with him yesterday, but he didn't turn up. He thought David had forgotten.'

Since they had moved to Nevis Drive, David had had a job selling car-insurance, which meant he had to travel all over Strathclyde.

'He must have had an accident, Mum!' Lucy cried, remembering how fast David sometimes drove. She felt sick, partly because she was empty, partly through worry about David.

'No,' said her mother quickly, 'Mr Tomney checked with the police and the hospitals last night, and again this morning. There has been no report of any accident involving David.'

Why did Lucy have the feeling that her mother was hiding something from her? She waited silently, giving her a chance to say more. But Mrs Bell sat without speaking, staring into the dead fire.

'What will we do, Mum?' Lucy asked.

Her mother raised her head slowly as though she were in a dream. 'There's nothing much we can do, except wait,' she said. 'David may phone at any minute. Or he may walk in and explain everything.' Then her voice became brisker. 'But you mustn't worry about it, Lucy,' she said. 'This is our problem: David's and mine.'

Lucy wished her mother would stop saying

that. She couldn't help worrying about David. She was very fond of him, though this hadn't always been the case. She and David had been at loggerheads for about a year after he moved in with Mum. But when Mrs Bell had gone into hospital to have Reuben, they had been forced to call a truce. Lucy had learned a lot about David in that week. She had heard all about his headmaster-father and his schoolteacher-mother who had wanted him to be a doctor, or a lawyer, or a teacher. She had heard how disappointed they had been, when David kept failing his university examinations, and how furious they were when he finally gave up his studies to be a bus-driver.

'They drove me to the verge of a nervous breakdown,' he told Lucy bitterly. 'I'll never do that to my son . . . or to you, Lucy,' he had added, to show Lucy that her future mattered to him too.

Nowadays, Lucy referred to David as 'my stepfather', because that was how she thought of him. They enjoyed games of Scrabble and Monopoly together, and often joined forces to amuse Reuben when he was bored and Mrs Bell was busy. She loved him just as much as if he were her real dad. Where on earth could he have got to? He had behaved quite normally at breakfast yesterday, which was the last time she had seen him. Suddenly she realized she was on the verge of tears. It was a relief when the door burst open and Reuben came staggering in from the lobby to fling himself down on the hearthrug.

'Mummy, Mummy!' he yelled, rolling over on to his back. 'I've had a dreadful, dreadful accident. I crashed on the last bend. The engine's on fire. And I'm drastically injured. The doctors want to excavate my leg.'

17

'Oh, no!' cried Mrs Bell, looking at him in alarm. 'You mustn't let them amputate, Reuben. You'll never drive in a race again if they do.'

Lucy had a sinking feeling as though she were going down in a lift. Mum liked Reuben to think she took his make-believe seriously. But for her to talk like that now, when they were so worried about David . . . It made Lucy wonder if she wasn't just a bit potty!

She studied her mother covertly as she and Reuben continued an earnest discussion about his chances of becoming World Motor-Racing Champion this year. The truth of the matter was, Mum was rather peculiar. She had a lot of odd habits, apart from wearing long dresses. For example she often rode around Old Whitefields on a large, ancient bike with no gears, holding up the buses as she pedalled creakily up the hills. People stared at her, not because of her creaky knees, but because, in Old Whitefields, bikes were for kids. No one over eighteen years of age rode one.

Then there was her hair, hanging straight to her waist, like Rapunzel's. Had it been golden, or raven-black, it might have looked all right. But it was a muddy brown, mixed with grey. And the grey was becoming more noticeable every month because Mum refused to use a colour rinse like other mothers did. She said she wasn't ashamed of being a mature woman. It didn't seem to strike her that waist-length grey hair made people think of witches. Some rude little kids had actually yelled, 'Winnie Witch!' after her, the day she had marched up and down the Big Green with Reuben, scattering her wildflower seeds. Lucy, who had been watching from a safe distance, had been mortified.

Lucy's heart gave a lurch. Was this why David

had cleared off: because Mum embarrassed him too? It was quite possible. No one ever stared at David. He was too ordinary. He dressed like everyone else, he went to football matches on Saturdays, watched snooker on television and washed his car on Sundays like all the other dads. He wasn't like Marmion Bell, Lucy's dead father. Marmion had been a poet with the same kind of artistic temperament as Mum.

Marmion Bell had been six-foot-two with shoulder-length black hair and eyes as blue as cornflowers. Mum and he had met when they were taking part in a Festival of Arts in St Andrews, she playing the piano, and he reading his poetry. When they had married, they had bought an old, half-ruined cottage on the island of Harasay in the Hebrides. They had made it weatherproof, taken up crofting, and had filled their little home with music and poetry. Marmion had always worn the kilt. He had been the last of the Great Romantics, Mum said. His choice of a name for his baby daughter was proof of this. Lucy, whose middle name was Ashton, was called after the heroine of Sir Walter Scott's *Bride of Lammermoor*.

David Darcy had thought Lucy was called after a Clyde paddle-steamer, when he first heard her name. That showed how totally unpoetical he was and how unlike Marmion Bell. David didn't like Mum acting in a way that made people stare. Perhaps he had indeed had enough.

Mrs Bell's large dark eyes left Reuben and settled on Lucy. She gave her daughter a smile full of gentleness. Suddenly Lucy ached with love for her. What had she been thinking of? David would never want to leave Mum. She was a warm, caring, marvellous human being.

'Lucy, pet, you'd better eat some breakfast if you're going out with Fiona,' her mother said. 'You know how busy the town is on a Saturday morning. You'll be jostled and knocked about. And you'll need your strength if you've to cope with a Donald choosing shoes. They're a family who seem incapable of making up their minds. Every time I meet Mrs Donald she's off to exchange something she bought the day before in Marks & Spencer's. So at least have coffee and a slice of toast.'

'All right, Mum,' Lucy said.

She ran to give her mother a hug before going through to the kitchenette. As she shoved a slice of bread under the grill, she could hear Mum describing to Reuben the route he ought to take if he was going to travel from Glasgow to Le Mans by car.

3

David Turns Up

As Lucy banged the garden gate shut behind her just before eleven, Old Hamish's door was yanked open and his head poked out. Lucy thought he looked like the convict in the old movie of *Great Expectations*, rising up from behind the gravestones.

'Hey, you! Lulu!' he shouted huskily.

Old Hamish had called her Lulu from the first day they moved into number ten. Lucy didn't know whether he had misheard her name when she was introduced to him, or whether this was just another of his many peculiar ways.

He beckoned to her to come back. 'Are you going into town?' he asked.

'Yes, Mr Henderson. Is there something you want?' she said politely. She hoped it was nothing from the off-licence. Mum had told him again and again that Lucy wasn't allowed to buy alcohol, but he still kept asking her.

It was all right this morning, though. He just wanted a copy of *Exchange and Mart*. He got one nearly every week, but he wouldn't order it from the local newsagent because of the delivery-charge.

He counted the coins out with trembling fingers into Lucy's palm, his chest wheezing like a concertina. 'And don't you forget it, now!' he said with a scowl. 'And don't be losing any of my money, either.' He smelt like a pub, and his dressing-gown clearly needed a wash.

'No, Mr Henderson. I'll be careful,' Lucy said with a long-suffering sigh.

Old Hamish was always rude to women. Mum said he was what was called a 'misogynist'. Mrs McIver from number six reckoned some flighty girl had broken his heart in his youth which was why he had gone to sea and became so sour. But old Mrs Hood at number four said it was the fault of Bessie Henderson, Hamish's elder sister. He'd lived with her after he retired, and up until she died, four years ago, she'd led him a dog's life.

Whatever the reason, Hamish only spoke to Lucy and her mother when he needed something. But he was quite matey with David. And Reuben had an open invitation to go upstairs whenever he wanted, to look at all the curios the old man had collected during his years as a sailor.

Although Lucy ran all the way down Nevis Drive and along Whitefields Road, it was past eleven when she reached the bus terminus. To her disgust she saw no one waiting at the stop. That could mean only one thing. The bus had left on time and Fiona had caught it. Blast! Old Hamish had ruined her morning. Now she would just have to go home to sit with Mum and worry about David.

She was turning back despondently when she heard a yell, and there, to her surprise, was Fiona, dancing and waving on the other side of the road while she waited for a gap in the traffic.

Whitefields Road was the boundary between Old Whitefields and New Whitefields where

22

Fiona lived. They were both housing-schemes. But Old Whitefields belonged to the Macindoe Housing Company, and New Whitefields to the Corporation.

There were other differences too. Old Whitefields had been there since the Ice Age, whereas New Whitefields had been built only twenty years ago. Because the newer houses had flat roofs like hutches, the Old Whitefields tenants referred contemptuously to the other scheme as 'Bunnyland'. The New Whitefields folk had retaliated by naming the fifty-year-old scheme 'Toytown'.

Whitefields Comprehensive School had been built in Torridon Road in Old Whitefields. But it drew its pupils from both Bunnyland and Toytown. In the beginning there had been fights between the two groups. But nowadays the old rivalries were forgotten.

'Sorry I'm late, Lucy. We'll have to catch the eleven-twenty,' Fiona gasped as she bounded on to the pavement beside Lucy.

Fiona had freckles even in the winter-time, and brown, slightly bulgy eyes that gave her the same permanently anxious look as her mother and sister.

'I couldn't decide what to wear,' she said. 'Do you think this skirt's all right? It's not too baggy? Does it go with my jacket?'

'Great,' said Lucy shortly. She didn't even glance at the skirt. Fiona's constant preoccupation with how she looked irritated Lucy when she had problems on her mind.

'Do you think my hair's all right?' asked Fiona. 'It's not too flat?' She began to draw her fingers wildly through her hair to make it stand up in spikes.

Lucy noticed an old lady who had just arrived

23

at the terminus suddenly wheeling about and walking quickly on to the next stop. She probably thought Fiona had nits, or that she was a crazy adolescent about to run amok.

'Let's sit at the back upstairs,' said Fiona when the bus finally arrived. 'We can comb our hair there without anyone seeing us.'

As soon as they were settled, Lucy said quickly, 'Something awful happened this morning, Fiona. You know that speech we had to learn by heart for the Shakespeare lesson on Tuesday? It stuck to the bottom of my spot-lotion bottle. The whole page is a total write-off.'

She had been hoping to take Fiona's mind off her hair, and she certainly succeeded.

'Oh, Lucy! It *isn't*! That's *awful*! And Aggie's taking us for Shakespeare now. What on earth will you *do*? Will you confess?'

Fiona looked and sounded as though it was Reuben's head Lucy had torn off.

Lucy assumed a nonchalant air.

'No panic,' she said. 'We're in Aggie's room with the student on Monday. It should be easy enough to sneak another copy of the *Dream* out of the book-cupboard.'

'Talking of the student, have you done your essay for her?' Fiona asked, as the bus leapt into motion and threw them both against the seat in front.

'Essay? Oh, no! I'd forgotten all about it. I can't even remember the title,' wailed Lucy, rubbing a bruised knee.

She had been class monitor last week and had had to miss the last five minutes of the student's Monday lesson to take the Football Pavilion money to the office. But Miss Darroch, the student, never let anyone slip her net. If there was

24

an absentee, their best friend was always detailed to tell them what the homework was. Fiona had done so conscientiously. But Lucy had forgotten to write it down in her homework book.

'The title's *"My Hero"*. And I'm doing Bob Geldof. So you can't have him,' Fiona said quickly.

Lucy groaned. Yes. She remembered now. She had thought then it was a wet title. She did still. It was the kind that teachers in the primary school gave out, expecting the kids to write about William Wallace or Robert the Bruce. Miss Darroch was a menace. You never knew where you were with her. One minute she was acting like Mary Poppins. The next she had turned into She-Who-Must-Be-Obeyed. Lucy could imagine her being really nasty if people didn't hand their essays in on time.

'Do you remember the students who came to your primary school?' she asked Fiona suddenly.

Fiona nodded, her eyes far away.

'The ones who came to my primary schools were lovely girls,' Lucy said nostalgically. 'We used to cry when they left. I can't imagine anyone crying for Darroch. The students we've had this term have been as bad as the teachers.'

'I wouldn't mind red ones,' said Fiona pensively.

'What?'

'Shoes,' said Fiona. 'Red shoes might be fun for a change. Or blue, maybe . . . Or should I play safe and stick to black?'

Lucy didn't answer her. She stared morosely out of the window at the faded February greens of the grass and bushes in the park, convinced this weekend would be a washout.

* * *

As soon as Lucy turned into Nevis Drive at four o'clock that afternoon, she saw David's red Cavalier car parked outside their house. Immediately she forgot she was starving with hunger, that her feet were aching, and that she had quarrelled with Fiona in Lewis's and had come home from town on her own. A feeling of relief swept over her as though she had been hobbling around all afternoon with a stone in her shoe and had just shaken it out.

She ran up the hill and along the garden path, stopping briefly to shove Old Hamish's *Exchange and Mart* through his letter-box. Once inside her own door she tiptoed along the lobby, intending to burst into the living-room and make Reuben scream. Once he had been frightened out of his wits, she could give him the painting book she had bought him. She had always to go through this strange ritual when she came home from shopping in town. Reuben loved it.

Suddenly she stopped and looked up at the ceiling. Small feet were running, pit-pat, pit-pat, along Old Hamish's lobby. Then jumping down the two steps outside his bathroom door, thump, thump! That must be Reuben.

She could hear Mum and David now, talking in the living-room. Had David just arrived home? Were they talking privately? Was that why Reuben had been sent up to Old Hamish's?

Lucy hovered uncertainly outside the living-room door. Without meaning to, she found herself eavesdropping.

'David! David!' Mrs Bell was saying in a distressed voice. 'How could you lose a thousand pounds? A hundred I might understand. But not a thousand!'

'I know. I can't understand it myself.' David's

26

voice was tired and crackly, like an old man's. 'I just can't seem to come to terms with money, Laura. I should never have taken this job. I kept forgetting to pay in the customers' cash. Then I suppose I must have spent it without meaning to. I could see that my books were getting into a dreadful muddle, and I kept planning to straighten them out. But the muddle got worse and worse. Finally I couldn't face it. I just had to take off.'

'Oh, my poor David!' Mrs Bell cried. 'I can just imagine you worrying yourself sick in secret. And sleeping in the car like that beside Loch Lomond. Oh, you poor, silly man! What a daft way to have gone on! But the main thing is you've come back. And you've seen Mr Tomney. Now at least you know what needs to be done,' she finished more calmly.

'Aye,' said David in a flat voice. 'It's a miracle I need, Laura. Nothing else will save me.'

'Don't talk like that,' said Mrs Bell. 'Tomney's given us till April to find the money. The situation isn't hopeless.'

Lucy pushed the living-room door open. She was trembling with shock and fury.

'And what happens if you can't find the money?' she demanded, glaring at David.

'Lucy!' her mother began angrily. 'You've no right to . . .'

But David lifted his hand to silence her. He looked Lucy straight in the eye.

'I'll go to jail, pet,' he said quietly. 'I expect you think I deserve to.'

Lucy said nothing. She looked from David to her mother in despair. Then she rushed past them both to lock herself in her room.

4

The Family in Trouble

Lucy would not come out of her room, not even
when David called to her in a tight voice that he
had made her spaghetti bolognaise and she must
come and eat it before it got cold. Neither would
she come out when her mother, gamely trying to
sound cheerful, shouted that she needed Lucy to
turn the pages while she played Chopin waltzes
to Reuben before his bedtime, nor even when
Reuben himself rattled the door handle for a full
five minutes, pathetically chanting his sister's
name.

She was hungry and thirsty and cold. But she
would rather be that than have to sit looking at
David, pretending that she didn't hate him for
what he had done.

There came a point, however, when she simply
had to go to the lavatory. But she was determined
she wasn't going to walk through the living-
room. Climbing out of her window she ran round
the house and crept in at the front door as
stealthily as a burglar. She returned to her room
by the same route. Then, pulling the curtains, she
switched on the light, hoisted herself up on to her
bed, and sat staring blindly at the wall.

At half past seven her mother tapped on the
door. 'Darling! You must eat something,' she

called anxiously. 'Missing meals gives you stomach ulcers. I know that from bitter experience, and you might bring on a migraine attack.'

'I'm not hungry. I feel sick,' Lucy told her in a trembling voice. She hoped that David would hear her. She hoped he was feeling sick – with guilt and shame.

Mrs Bell gave a groaning sort of sigh and left. There was a murmur of voices. Then Lucy heard the television being switched on. So! Mum couldn't spare any more time for her daughter, it seemed, no matter how unhappy she was.

Lucy lay face down on her bed and tears filled her eyes. She thought about all she had had to put up with in the past few years. How, just when she had settled into a school, Mum and David would decide to move house again. She had been to three different primary schools: in Dumfries, Lothian and Strathclyde. And before she came to Whitefields, she had had a year and a bit at Westbank Comprehensive on the other side of Glasgow. No wonder she was behind in her maths and French! And she had never yet had a proper school uniform, because there were always bits of the last school's uniform she had to wear out. After a year at Whitefields she was still wearing a grey Westbank skirt instead of a navy Whitefields one.

It never seemed to occur to Mum either that Lucy might want to go on a school trip, like the ten days' skiing holiday in North Italy, or the week in London. It was never even suggested. Mum had made it plain enough that she had found it difficult to scrape up even the five pounds Lucy had needed for the two-day drama workshop last term.

What was it they said about money? That it

was the root of all evil? It certainly was in this household when idiots like Mum and David were in charge of it. Living with them was like having a permanent berth on the Titanic. And now the iceberg had struck.

Lucy's nose was beginning to run. She reached down and began to poke about in the muddle on the floor, hoping to unearth a packet of paper tissues. Suddenly she found herself staring at a glossy, coloured photograph that had been taken three years ago at a steam museum they had visited. David had asked a man who was passing to take the photograph so they would all be in it. Reuben beamed up at her, curly-haired and chubby. Mum was wearing the long black-and-white skirt she had bought at the Tree Fair that summer. She had an arm round Lucy's shoulders. Lucy was holding David's hand. Fiona Donald always said David looked like Prince Andrew with a moustache. True enough, in this photograph he did.

It had been a super day. Lucy remembered it vividly. David had suggested the outing in the first place to cheer Mum up as he had just been made redundant again. As well as the steam engines, there had been a couple of sideshows and David had won a white furry toy mouse for her. She still had it on top of her wardrobe. She picked the photograph up and turned it over. Someone (probably Mum) had printed 'Happy Family' on the back in neat, black letters.

Lucy's eyes had filled again while she was remembering that day at the museum. Now, hot tears spilled over and ran down her cheeks. She really was feeling sick – sick with herself. She jumped down from the bed and ran across to look in the dressing-table mirror. She didn't look any different. Her nose still looked as though some-one had chopped it off short. Her eyes were far too big for that silly wee white face. And you could still see those awful streaks in her hair. But she hadn't grown horns yet. She didn't *look* like a monster, even though she had been acting like one.

She found a grubby tissue in her bag and wiped her eyes and blew her nose. Then, quietly and methodically, she set about tidying her room. She emptied every drawer and cupboard first so that she could start from scratch. It took her ages. She had almost finished when her mother called from the living-room, 'Don't stay up too late, dear. It's quarter to eleven. David's off to Dundee in the morning, so don't worry if you hear us up and about very early.'

'Good night!' Lucy called in an extra cheerful voice, to show she had got over her sulks. 'See you in the morning.'

She waited for a bit, then quietly unlocked her door. She opened it wide so that a panel of light fell across the floor of the darkened room. Then she tiptoed across to press down the light switch.

As she had guessed, the dishes from the evening meal still lay, unwashed, on the table. Mum forgot about things like dirty dishes when she was worrying about money. Lucy piled them together and carried them through to the kitch-enette. When she switched on the light there, she found three dirty pans in the sink. She pushed up the sleeves of her sweater, filled the sink with hot water, added a squirt of washing-up liquid, and set to work. It was nearly midnight by the time the kitchen was clean and tidy, and the table in the living-room was laid for Sunday morning's breakfast.

Suddenly Lucy realized how hungry she was.

31

She poured some milk into a mug and made two thick marmalade sandwiches. She felt better when she had eaten them, but she was terribly tired. Coming back from the bathroom she found herself bouncing off the walls of the lobby, the way Old Hamish did when he was drunk. But when she finally lay down to sleep, she felt as cool and peaceful as though she had just come out of a fever. She had recovered from the shock of David's revelation, though she was still frightened when she thought about the worrying weeks that now lay ahead. But she didn't hate David any more. And she was no longer angry with her mother. They were her family. And you had to be on your family's side. You had to support them.

5

Jackdaw Reuben

By the time Lucy woke next morning, David had left for Dundee to see if his parents or his sisters would lend him any money. None of them had spoken to him for a year after Reuben's birth because they thought it a disgrace for people to have babies if they weren't married. David had waited until Reuben had dimples and curly hair. Then he had taken him to Dundee to thaw out the Darcys. His trip had been a partial success. Reuben had broken the ice. But only for himself and David. Mum and Lucy were still not welcome.

'I do hope he drives carefully. He has so much on his mind and it's always an ordeal for him to visit his father,' Mrs Bell said as Lucy came out of her room. 'I suppose I really ought to have gone with him. Why didn't I think of it?'

Her arms were folded and she was pacing back and forward between the living-room window and the door of the kitchenette. Lucy noticed that, in her agitation, she had put on her long Black Watch skirt inside out. She hurried over and put an arm round her mother's shoulders.

'But, Mum! If you had gone with David, it would only have given him one more thing to worry about. He would have been wondering all the way how the Darcys would behave to you when you arrived,' Lucy pointed out.

'You're right, darling! Of course you are.' Mrs Bell squeezed Lucy's hand gratefully. 'You're a very sensible girl for your age,' she said. 'And thank you for tidying up so nicely in here. It made all the difference to poor David's breakfast. It showed him that you had forgiven him.'

Lucy nodded in the direction of Reuben's room, where her brother could be heard playing a jazzed-up version of 'Baa, baa, black sheep' on his recorder.

'Shall I go and help him to dress?' she asked.

'Oh, yes please!' said Mrs Bell. 'He's quite capable of dressing himself. But he keeps going off into a daydream. After breakfast I'll take him up to the Big Green to give Rufus a run. I've been promising him all week I'd do that.'

Rufus was Reuben's imaginary dog – a cross between a Great Dane and a Red Setter from his master's description. He was much too large for a small house and was constantly being trodden on or squashed. This morning, because he was lying across Reuben's threshold, Lucy unknowingly walked right across his middle, causing Reuben to scream and hurl his recorder at her.

Lucy fell to the ground, groaning, pretending to be badly hurt, and Reuben came flying across to fling his arms round her neck. He was still in his vest and pants, and his arms and legs felt icy. Lucy hurriedly shoved him into his blue cord jeans and sweater, then held him at arm's length to inspect him. He looked at her coyly from beneath his long lashes. He was a good-looking little boy, she thought. But he behaved in a really odd way sometimes. Were all four-year-old boys like him? she wondered. Or had Reuben inherited some of Mum's weirdness?

'I've just told Rufus to bite your leg to the bone if you don't say you're sorry,' he announced with a sweet smile.

'OK. Sorry, Fleabag!' Lucy called amiably over her shoulder.

She stared disapprovingly at Reuben's jeans. They were beginning to droop already and give him corrugated legs. Mum had bought them at the 'Good as New' shop last week and they were a size too large. She grabbed Reuben by the waistband and tried to hitch the trousers up. As she did so something fell from his back pocket and clattered on to the floor.

Reuben made a dive for it, but Lucy was quicker. She picked up the object and peered at it suspiciously. It certainly wasn't a toy. It was a kind of ornament by the look of it. It was like the Chinese soapstone Buddhas Gran Campbell put in her display cabinet, only it was yellower. And it wasn't a Buddha. It was more like an evil-looking garden gnome carrying a spear and a shield, and riding a pony. She could see why it attracted Reuben. The gnome was revolting, but the pony was cute. It was like a Shetland, with sturdy little legs and a fringe down to its eyes.

Lucy looked at Reuben sternly. 'Where did this come from?' she demanded.

She was pretty sure she knew the answer, but she was determined to make Reuben sweat a bit to teach him a lesson.

He didn't say a word. His mouth fell open and he stared vacantly at her hand.

'Come on!' Lucy demanded. 'Out with it! Where did you get this?' She grabbed her brother by the back of his neck and held the ornament up in front of him. Nevertheless, she didn't want her mother to hear what was going on, so she had to keep her voice low, which made it difficult for her to be properly outraged.

'Don't know! Leave me go, Lucy!' Reuben jerked his head from side to side, trying to shake her off.

'Well, *I* know,' said Lucy decisively. 'It came from Old Hamish's. Didn't it?'

Silence.

'Did Old Hamish give it to you?'

Silence.

'I see. He didn't give it to you. That means you stole it. You're a thief. You stole from a poor old-age pensioner. You're horrible and disgusting. You're a bad, wicked wee boy!'

'Didn't steal it . . . ' Reuben's lower lip trembled. He tried unsuccessfully to kick Lucy on the shin. 'Rufus found it,' he said with sudden inspiration. 'He wouldn't drop it. I had to let him bring it home.'

'Little fibber! Rufus did not!'

'Did so!'

'Did not!'

'Did!' Reuben suddenly tore himself free and ran to the door, where he stepped carefully over Rufus's tail before turning round to stick his tongue out.

Lucy decided to try another tack. 'Where did Rufus find it?' she asked sharply.

'Behind Old Hamish's wardrobe. In his bedroom,' Reuben answered readily.

'I see.' Lucy stared coldly at the spot where Rufus seemed to be stretched out. 'Well, if he ever does such a thing again, I'll have to tell the police,' she said. 'And he will be *destroyed*.'

Reuben swallowed hard, grabbed Rufus's

invisible collar, and hauled him off to the living-room.

Lucy sighed. She hoped Reuben wasn't growing into one of those problem children people talked about. He had been going through what Mum called 'a jackdaw stage' for about a month now. They had found his nursery school teacher's lipstick at the bottom of his satchel. Then he'd hidden Mrs McIver's clothes-peg bag under his bed. And the last time Lucy had taken him to see the Donalds, he had tried to smuggle out Ailsa's styling-brush under his jacket.

Suddenly Lucy had a terrifying thought. What if there was a criminal streak in the Darcy family? Maybe you started off with soapstone gnomes and finished up embezzling insurance money. Was poor Reuben fated to end his days in Barlinnie prison?

But that was rubbish! Lucy's face turned scarlet, just as if David had been standing in front of her reading her mind. David wasn't a criminal. He was just hopeless at dealing with money. So was Mum. It was a pity they had teamed up together. They each should have found a responsible person to manage their finances for them. You had to feel sorry for them, even if their stupidity made you furious at times.

She shoved the ornament into the back pocket of her jeans. She would give it back to Old Hamish this afternoon. He never got up until midday on a Sunday. He had probably never missed it anyway. And there was no need for her to tell Mum that Reuben had been 'jackdawing' again. She had enough to worry about at the moment.

Half an hour later Lucy stood on the doorstep watching Reuben and her mother setting off up

Nevis Drive for the Big Green. Reuben's right arm was stuck stiffly out in front of him, holding Rufus's invisible lead. Every now and again Mum would bend over and make patting motions in the air. A group of elderly women on their way back from church turned to stare at her. Lucy suddenly remembered she hadn't told her mother that she had her skirt on inside out. She only hoped that no one she knew would be on the Big Green this morning!

In the afternoon Lucy shut herself in her room to write her essay for the student. She lay on her bed with her exercise book on her stomach, sucked the end of her biro, and waited for inspiration. Half an hour passed with no results. She felt very drowsy. If she wasn't careful she might fall asleep and not wake up for hours. She'd better find a hero to write about quickly. It was a pity Fiona had bagged Bob Geldof. Maybe she would have to fall back on Robert the Bruce and his corny spider after all.

The noises off weren't helping her concentration. Reuben was bawling out nursery-rhymes at the top of his voice as he kicked his football against the wall beneath her window. And goodness knows what was going on upstairs! It sounded as though Old Hamish had invited an elephant in to demonstrate the Highland Fling. She had never heard such a banging and crashing up there before. To top it all, Mum was in her bedroom fiddling like mad to soothe her nerves. She had started with Bach. Now she was on to Vivaldi. Lucy couldn't play an instrument, but she had listened to so much music that she could usually identify a composer within a few bars.

How had her father, Marmion Bell, managed

to write his poetry with Mum playing music all day in their tiny Hebridean cottage, Lucy wondered. It must have been very difficult for him.

Suddenly Lucy sat up straight. Of course! Why hadn't she thought of it before? Her own father had been a hero. A real hero. She would write about him. She would describe how Marmion Bell had died through saving her and Mum from the fire. She hadn't heard the story for years. Not since David had come to live with them. But Mum had told it to her so often when she was small that it was printed indelibly on her memory.

Lucy opened her exercise-book. Her pen began to fly across the page. English was her best subject. Mum had once said this was a legacy to her from her father. Her short, stubby fingers could never hope to make music like her mother's. But they could write essays she needn't feel ashamed of.

It took the rest of the afternoon and half the evening to write the account of her father's heroic death – how, in the little cottage on Harasay, a fire had started in the chip-pan on the range, and had spread to a line of Lucy's nappies drying above it; how Marmion Bell had dived through the flames to get into the back room, where Mum had been bathing Lucy; how he had soaked blankets in the bath water to wrap round them before carrying them to safety; and how, badly burned as he was, he had run two miles in the snow for help, catching pneumonia as a result and dying four days later. She described how his life's work, his Collected Poems, which he had been about to post off to his publisher, had gone up in smoke with all their other worldly possessions.

When Lucy had finished writing, she sat

staring ahead of her, her fingers feeling through her thick hair for the scar above her temple, where the flames had licked her head. She didn't think much about her father nowadays, she realized guiltily. Marmion Bell ought to be remembered by his own flesh and blood. After all, every line of his work had been destroyed. He had no blood-relatives that Mum knew of, apart from Lucy, because he'd been an orphan, brought up in a Home. And all the photographs of him had been burned, along with all the family documents, in the fire. The only way his memory would live on was in the hearts of the two who had been closest to him.

At ten o'clock she roused herself and went through to the kitchenette to make cocoa for herself and her mother. They drank it in silence. Mum's dark eyes were far away. Her head nodded now and again as though she were holding an imaginary conversation with someone. Suddenly she got up and crossed to the piano and began softly picking out the first notes of the slow movement of Beethoven's Fourth Piano Concerto. It was at a performance of this that she met David. They regarded it as their special music.

Lucy stared at her mother sitting brooding over the piano keys, her hair falling over her shoulders like a cape. Mum's thoughts were with David in Dundee. That was obvious. There was no room in her heart any more for poor Marmion Bell. Lucy was the only one left in the world who wanted to remember him.

6

A Disastrous Day

Normally, Lucy didn't set off for school until ten to nine. On this Monday morning, however, because David wasn't at home, she had first to take Reuben to his nursery school which was at the end of Whitefields Road. The three of them – Lucy, Reuben, and Mum – left the house together at twenty past eight, Mum swinging her violin-case.

It was a cold, bright morning with a biting wind and scudding clouds.

'Can't you smell the spring, children?' their mother asked, stopping to throw her head back and breathe deeply.

Then she sighed and her shoulders drooped as her springy walk changed to a plod. To begin with Lucy thought she must be worrying about David. But it turned out she was thinking about the pupils she had to teach that day.

'That great clumsy Mary McRae,' she suddenly burst out. 'They'd be better to have her take lessons for the musical saw . . . And the boy, Burns! He's impossible. I'll never do anything with him.'

She waved to them absent-mindedly at the foot of Nevis Drive where their ways parted, then ran after them to kiss Reuben. She didn't look too

41

bad this morning, Lucy noted with relief, even though she was wearing her long brown skirt and black cape. The wind had whipped up the red in her cheeks and was making her eyes sparkle. If it hadn't been for the grey hair, she might almost have passed for pretty.

'Goodbye! Goodbye! Take care, children,' she called anxiously after them as though they were setting off up the Amazon instead of walking to the end of the road.

Lucy hated walking along Whitefields Road at this time in the morning. On the New Whitefields side there was a continuous stream of traffic heading for the Industrial Estate which lay under the railway-bridge beyond the terminus. And alongside the pavement where Lucy and Reuben were walking, buses and cars zoomed by at five-second intervals on their way to the city. But it wasn't just the noise that troubled Lucy. Last term an environmentalist had come to talk to 3A and had told the class how much lead was still being spewed out by petrol-driven engines and how it was probably damaging people's brains.

Anyone watching Reuben might have thought the lead was working on him already, for he was staring fixedly ahead, doing a kind of goose-step.

'The motor cars whizz by,
They whizz by faster and faster,
Reuben walks,
Lucy walks,
But Rufus is tied in his kennel,'
he chanted over and over at the top of his voice.

Mum made a point of always praising Reuben when he recited one of his daft songs. Lucy didn't. And this morning she decided he must be positively discouraged, since they were rapidly approaching the Bought Houses.

'Reuben! Will you *shut up*!' she yelled.

The Bought Houses (they were never referred to in any other way locally) were three-dozen bungalows, even older than Toytown, that huddled together near the end of Whitefields Road. Their owners regarded themselves as being several cuts above the common mortals from the two housing-schemes. It was not out of respect for these superior beings' feelings, though, that Lucy had offended Reuben. It was because she did not want to look like an idiot (or an idiot's big sister) when they were passing number 326. This was the bungalow Mum called 'Elizabethan Eyesore', because of its mock-Tudor timbering and eaves. It was the home of The Great Douglas Gordon.

Douglas (who, Lucy imagined, looked just as Marmion Bell must have done at seventeen) captained Whitefields School football, swimming, squash and tennis teams. But he wasn't just a brilliant sportsman. He was brainy, too – so brainy that he was going to stay on at school for an extra year to be coached for the University Bursary Examination. Probably ninety per cent of the girls in the school thought they were in love with him.

Last autumn Lucy and Fiona Donald had walked up and down this stretch of Whitefields Road almost every evening, like two policewomen pounding a beat, until Fiona's interfering brother, Rory, had found out about it, and had told them scornfully to lay off. Rory was in the Fifth Form and was a reserve for the First Eleven football team. His freckles were even more numerous than Fiona's and he had tight, red, woolly curls. He thought he was a genius, Fiona said, because he had been accepted by some uppity chess-club in Pollokshields. Lucy couldn't stand him.

A quick glance at Pooh's tummy showed Lucy it was almost eight-forty. So it was possible that Douglas might emerge at any moment. Her heart began to bang in her ears. She deliberately slowed her step as they drew level with the Elizabethan Eyesore's hedge, at the same time whispering to Reuben that she would kill him if he didn't stop digging his nails into her palm. They walked past the gate of number 326 at a funereal pace. But there was no sign of Douglas.

Nor did Lucy see him when she passed the bungalow again ten minutes later, having left Reuben stamping round the church-hall singing his daft song to some other poor kids who had arrived early. As she turned up Ratagan Drive and joined the stream of navy blazers now flowing uphill towards Torridon Road, Lucy wondered whether not seeing Douglas was a bad omen. Did it mean that, for today, the Fates were not on her side? Lucy was a firm believer in omens, Fate, astrology and suchlike. Mum had once told her that Marmion Bell had been just the same.

To begin with it seemed that the day would not turn out too badly after all. The Head, who was a sports fanatic, became quite emotional at assembly when he read out the results of the Saturday sports-fixtures. Whitefields First Eleven football team had beaten Bellmoss High (a snooty, fee-paying school) by ten goals to one, Douglas Gordon having scored six of the goals. A great cheer went up and every head turned towards Douglas who stood, nodding and smiling, in the line of prefects by the side of the platform.

A lump came into Lucy's throat, and she found herself gazing at Douglas through a mist. The emotion of the moment even broke down the wall of huffy silence there had been until then between Fiona and herself, the aftermath of Saturday's quarrel in Lewis's. As they left the hall, Fiona gripped Lucy's arm and whispered, 'I should have written about *him* in my essay, Lucy. Why on earth didn't I think of it?'

3A's week started with a double period of science. Until the end of last term Lucy had loathed these two hours on a Monday morning. But since January the New System had been in force. And it was great. The lab had been lined with drawers containing different-coloured cards with experiments printed on them. The pupils (either individually or in pairs) had to work their way through these, starting with the pale pink cards and finishing with the sickly green. While they worked, their teacher, Mr Young, sat disgruntled at his desk filling in *The Herald* crossword.

Lucy and Fiona, who worked together, hardly ever knew what they were supposed to be doing. Sometimes they were not even sure whether they were working at chemistry or at physics. They had no hope of ever leaving the pale pink drawer. But, unlike Mr Young, they were very happy with the New System. While they waited in queues for iron-filings, or for a Bunsen burner, they would chat about non-scientific matters and eat Fudgo bars. (Fiona's father was a supervisor in the Fudgo Sweet Factory on Whitefields Industrial Estate.) This morning they discussed ways in which Fiona could distract the student teacher while Lucy sneaked another copy of the *Dream* out of Aggie's book-cupboard. Lucy had intended making her foray at the start of the lesson, when Miss Darroch was collecting the essays. But Fiona favoured the end when the 'sooks' always crowded round the student to tell her they loved her new sweater, or to admire her engagement ring for the umpteenth time.

'Don't worry, pal! You'll bring it off,' Fiona declared with heartwarming confidence.

Lucy was sure she would, too. Her faith in herself was still unshaken by the mid-morning break when she, Fiona and Hazel Black (another Douglas Gordon fan) took up their usual positions outside the mobile classroom. From here they could gaze into the Prefects' Room in the main building and, if they were lucky, catch The Great Douglas's eye. This morning, however, they had to be content with a glimpse of his broad back and shoulders.

'I'm sure he winked at me at assembly,' Hazel whispered confidingly to the other two as the bell signalled the end of break.

Hazel wasn't exactly a raving beauty. For a start she had a jutting-out chin. But she was always imagining Douglas was looking at her. As the three of them shuffled into Aggie's room for their English lesson, Fiona gave Lucy a meaningful nudge. Lucy wasn't sure whether this signified, *Good luck in the book-snatch*! or *Isn't Hazel Black hilarious*? The next moment she didn't care.

'Move along there! Who *is* that blocking the doorway?' a stentorian voice behind them demanded.

The blast from it shot them all into their seats double-quick. The door was slammed shut. And Aggie McLintock herself strode across the floor and stood by her desk glaring at them.

'Miss Darroch has caught chicken-pox,' she started in an angry voice, as though it were somehow their fault.

Lucy, unnerved by Aggie's unexpected

appearance at what was to have been the scene of her crime, gave an hysterical whinny. The teacher's pale-blue eyes widened in a glassy stare of disbelief. Half-a-dozen steps carried her to where Lucy sat in the front row, next to the radiator.

'That girl with the colours in her hair, stand!' she barked.

She raised her arm to point at Lucy's head. In her black academic gown, with her scraped-back white hair, she looked like a lop-sided, geriatric Batman.

Lucy got to her feet, clinging to her desk for support. She wished she were dead. She wondered if all the others were already, for she could not hear anyone breathing.

'Do you find it amusing to hear of people falling ill?' Aggie asked in a deceptively gentle tone.

Lucy shook her head. She could guess what was coming next. Aggie's technique was notorious. Sure enough, the teacher suddenly put two hands on Lucy's desk, thrust her face forward, and said menacingly, 'Do you know me, girl?'

For thirty years this enigmatic challenge had instilled terror into the hearts of Aggie's pupils. None of them had ever been able to decide whether, 'Do you know me, girl?' or 'Do you know me, boy?' was a serious question. So no one had ever attempted to answer it. They had all stood, dumb and quaking, just like Lucy at this moment. It was rumoured that Aggie had put the same question to her husband a week after their wedding and she hadn't seen him since. Aggie's next line was, 'Because now *I* know *you*!'

Someone's stomach rumbled squeakily in the silence, but no one dared to laugh.

'Name?' snapped Aggie with a suddenness that made Lucy jump and bang her knee against the desk.

'Lucy Bell.'

'Ah . . . yes!'

Lucy was not flattered that the Head of English had obviously heard of her. The sneering note in Aggie's voice spoke of teachers gossiping in the staffroom about the girl whose weirdly-dressed mother lived with a man she wasn't married to. Lucy's cheeks burned with embarrassment.

'Try to behave less like an infant and more like a Third Former in future,' Aggie rasped out, at the same time signalling impatiently to Lucy to sit down. Her face had taken on the same expression as Reuben's when he suddenly became bored with his farm-animals and started chucking them into corners.

'Take out your *Interpretation and Précis* books,' she hollered to the room at large.

This was a terrible blow. Miss Darroch had promised to read another chunk from *The Lord of the Flies* today. She had stopped last week just where Roger, Ralph and Jack had seen the bulging creature on the mountain. The class had been looking forward to it all morning.

Alistair Scott, who sat in the middle of the back row and had owlish spectacles, shot up his hand to protest. But when he looked at Aggie's face, he changed his mind.

'P-please, Miss,' he stammered. 'We have an essay to hand in.'

Aggie looked at him with intense dislike. She had just lost her only free period of the day. Now she would have to cart twenty-eight Third Form essays home and read the puerile rubbish into the bargain.

'Lay your essay books on your desks,' she ordered them crossly.

Lucy fished hers out of her bag. As she straightened, she inadvertently caught the teacher's eye.

'Lucy Bell will collect them,' Aggie ordained.

Lucy sprang to her feet, falling over her bag in her haste. Being the only pupil in the class known to Aggie by name was a distinction she would rather have foregone. As she walked up and down the rows picking up the books, she reflected gloomily that now she hadn't a cat in hell's chance of getting near the book-cupboard. Which meant that tomorrow was bound to be even more of a disaster than today.

7

Lucy Gets a Fright

There was no one in when Lucy got home and the house was just as they had left it in the morning. Perhaps it was because she had had a bad day at school that she felt so depressed when she looked around her. The ashes were piled up in the fireplace. Reuben's pyjama trousers were still lying in the middle of the floor where he had dropped them. And the morning paper was draped over an unwashed coffee-mug on the table. You could tell it was Mum who had left it like that because it was open at the Entertainments page. She always liked to see what concerts she might have gone to if she had had any money to spare for tickets – which she never did.

Her mother rarely left Lucy a note to say where she had gone. Lucy usually had to work it out for herself. It didn't take a great detective to do that today. To begin with, David's leather jacket had come back from Dundee and was hanging on the handle of the cupboard door, so presumably David had come with it. Also the big shopping-trolley had gone from its corner next to the piano. Added to this the fact that Mum always shopped on Mondays if she could (since hardly anyone else did) it was reasonable then to suppose that the three other members of Lucy's family were at that moment at the Betterbrig Supermarket.

The living-room was cold. Lucy could have brought the radiator through from her bedroom, but she always tried to economize on electricity for fear of it being cut off again. She always felt sick for days after that happened. She decided she would have something to eat, and then light the fire. If it wasn't lit soon there would be no hot water to wash up the dishes after tea.

She went into the kitchenette and looked in the breadbin. It was empty apart from some green crumbs stuck in the corners. A search through the cupboards revealed two tins of carrots and three peculiar-looking onions with long green shoots like periscopes growing out of them. Honestly, Mum was a hopeless organizer! Mother Hubbard and she would have had a lot in common. Lucy angrily banged shut all the doors, made herself a cup of coffee with two big spoonfuls of sugar, and carried it through to her bedroom where she could snuggle under her quilt and keep warm.

She thought enviously of Fiona, no doubt lounging in her centrally-heated bedroom, watching her portable television, and stuffing herself with goodies. The Donalds always had stacks of food, no matter what day of the week it was. Plain and chocolate biscuits. All kinds of cakes and tarts. Buns. Oranges. Apples. Pears. Mountains of Fudgo bars. Their kitchen was like a miniature supermarket.

Lucy's stomach made a plaintive noise, more of a whine than a rumble. She had finished her coffee and she was still ravenous. She must stop thinking about food, she decided. She would change out of her school uniform and light the fire while she waited for the others. Perhaps they would stop off at the Chinese take-away, then she wouldn't have to wait for a meal to be cooked.

As she pulled her jeans on, something pricked her bottom and made her jump. She thought at first that a safety-pin had found its way into her back pocket, and had then unfastened itself in the treacherous way safety-pins have. But the next moment she was staring down at the ugly, yellow face of Old Hamish's pony-riding gnome. It was the pony's left ear that had dug into Lucy's bottom.

She ought to have taken it back yesterday, she thought guiltily. Not that she imagined that Old Hamish would be breaking his heart about it, even if he had missed it. The pony was all right. But the gnome was really repulsive. It looked as if it were dying to shove its spear into anyone who came within reach: its expression was positively maniacal. Where on earth had Old Hamish got it, she wondered. She couldn't believe that he had bought it. Perhaps it had been given to him by a relative. Her own family had been saddled with two hideous orange vases that Gran Campbell had given them. Mum kept them at the back of the living-room cupboard. Maybe Old Hamish's horrible, nagging sister, Bessie, had left the gnome to him in her will, out of spite.

At any rate she had better take it back to the old man right now, she decided, in case she forgot about it again. Her memory was less and less reliable these days. Not only had she forgotten about the essay for Miss Darroch. Now this. Maybe it was all because of the lead from the petrol-engines, wafting up from Whitefields Road and eating into her brain . . .

Lucy rang Old Hamish's doorbell twice. Then,

when there was still no answer, she knocked long and loudly.

She couldn't think why he insisted on keeping his bottom door locked in daylight when he was at home. None of the other upstairs tenants did. After all there was another door with a strong lock at the top of the inside staircase. If Lucy ever had to take a message to the McIvers at number six, she just ran straight upstairs and knocked at the top door. It saved a lot of time.

'Oh, come on! Come on!' she muttered impatiently when she had rung the bell for a third time to no effect. She hadn't taken time to pull on a jacket, and her sweater was no protection against a wind blowing straight from the snows of Ben Lomond.

Besides, she wanted to hand the gnome back before her family appeared. She was going to ask Old Hamish not to tell her mother what Reuben had done, since she had a lot on her mind at the moment.

She was just beginning another fusillade of knocking when Old Hamish yelled down to her from the top of the stairs. She couldn't make out all that he said, but what she did hear was pretty rude. He finished by threatening to string her up if she didn't stop her bloody racket.

Lucy groaned. It sounded as though the old man had been drinking again. What should she do? Just slip away back to her own house and give him the gnome later?

But he was already on his way down the stairs. She could hear the heavy thump as his boot hit each step, then the grunt as he gathered the strength to go on down to the next one. He would be absolutely furious if he arrived at the door to find no one there. Besides, he might guess that it had been Lucy and complain to her mother about her. Then she would have to spill the beans about Reuben.

She would just have to wait and see what sort of state Old Hamish was in. If he was too drunk, she wouldn't even try to explain what Reuben had done. She would just shove the gnome into his hands and run.

After what seemed an age the lock clicked back and the door opened slowly. She had never seen Old Hamish at close quarters when he was in the middle of a drinking bout. It was not a pleasant sight. He was wearing a raggedy, striped shirt with the sleeves rolled up showing scrawny old arms covered with faded tattoos. He looked as though he hadn't shaved for days, and his eyes were bleary and bloodshot. Still, he seemed compos mentis enough, judging from the way he greeted her.

'God's sake! I might have known it,' he wheezed. 'It had to be a wumman makin' all that din. *"Cherchez la femme."* Isn't that what they say, Lulu? When there's any trouble, look for the lady, eh? So what can I do for you, hen?'

He swayed forward and Lucy quickly backed down a step. The old man smelled awful – of sweaty armpits and whisky.

'I'm awfully sorry about this, Mr Henderson,' she started, holding the gnome out to him. 'But I'm afraid our Reuben . . . our Reuben . . . '

Lucy's voice faltered and died. Old Hamish was looking very queer. He was making a funny noise in his throat, and his whisky-flushed face had turned almost the colour of the gnome. Grabbing it out of her hand he hugged it to his chest. His eyes looked a bit like the gnome's, too.

Maniacal and staring. He was trying to say something, but the words wouldn't come out. Saliva was beginning to dribble down his stubbly chin.

Her stomach did a somersault. Was Old Hamish having some sort of fit? Drunkards did have fits. She had watched a television-documentary about it. They saw things like giant spiders and man-sized snails. Was Old Hamish seeing monsters now? She must keep calm, she told herself. It wouldn't help anyone if she panicked.

'Don't you feel well, Mr Henderson? Is there anything I can get you?' she asked in a shaky voice. To show her goodwill she stepped back on to the top step.

She was totally unprepared for what happened next.

Old Hamish's right arm shot out, grabbed the neckband of her sweater, and with surprising strength hauled her through the doorway. The next moment he had kicked the door shut and had Lucy pinned so hard against the staircase wall that the bannister almost broke her neck. His long, bony fingers dug into her shoulder. He was hurting her. Really hurting! His horrible, bloodshot eyes peered into her face.

'All right! Where did you get it?' he asked in a hoarse whisper. 'I want the truth, Lulu. Tell the truth and shame the devil. For if you don't, you'll rue the day. I'm warnin' you, now!'

Lucy was terrified. Old Hamish had gone off his rocker, and she was trapped in here with him. She could scream her head off and no one would hear her. The McIvers were away in Spain. Mrs Niven was at her son's home in Cornwall. There wasn't another soul in the whole building. She started to cry.

The colour flooded back into the old man's

face. He couldn't stand women crying. It put him in a fury. He started to shake Lucy angrily. He shook her till her teeth rattled.

'Will you answer me, you deceitful wee limmer?' he croaked. 'Where did you get my mannikin?'

Lucy finally found her courage and knocked Hamish's hand from her shoulder.

'You stop that! Just stop it now!' she sobbed. 'It was Reuben took your gnome. He found it behind your wardrobe. That's what I came to tell you. I wish I hadn't now. I wish I'd thrown it in the dustbin.'

'Reuben? Ah-h-h!' It was like the sigh people give if they've had a splinter removed or a painful boil squeezed, Lucy thought.

Old Hamish sat down heavily on the fourth stair from the bottom, still clutching the gnome in his left hand. He looked dazed.

'Behind the wardrobe,' he muttered thickly. 'Aye. I see now. It'll have fallen out of my box when I had it up on top. An' me turnin' the whole place upside down on Sunday lookin' for it!'

Lucy, seeing her chance of escape, lunged towards the door. But, quick as a flash, the old man's arm shot out. He caught Lucy's wrist in a pincer-like grip.

'Here!' he gasped agitatedly. 'Who else has seen the mannikin? Your mother? David?'

'No one else has seen it,' Lucy cried, on the verge of tears again. 'Only Reuben and me . . . Now, lay off, Mr Henderson! Do you hear me? If you don't, I'm going to start screaming. I'm warning you! And Mum and David will be back any minute.'

'Aye, aye,' Hamish muttered. He gave her wrist a last vicious squeeze. 'Not a word to anyone about me having that mannikin, now,' he growled, scowling at her ferociously. 'Not a whisper. It doesnae matter about the bairn. Nobody takes notice of what bairns say. But you hold your tongue, Lulu. Do you hear? I'll know if you've told anyone. I have ways of finding out.'

She managed to nod her head. If she had tried to speak, she would have started howling. Old Hamish Henderson was quite mad. She was convinced of it. He had an insane fixation about that horrible gnome. It was probably a form of drunkard's madness. Instead of seeing giant spiders he had an obsession about the yellow gnome. She would be lucky if she escaped in one piece.

But the next moment he released her wrist and pointed surlily towards the door. She was through it and at the bottom of the steps before he had struggled to his feet. She felt really sick. But she was shaking so hard, it was five minutes before she could hold a glass of water to her lips. In the end she made herself a cup of her mother's camomile tea, and did some deep-breathing for good measure. This did the trick. By the time the others arrived home, she was calmly lighting the fire.

But Lucy had come to a decision. Never – not for anything – was she going to go near that crazy old man upstairs again. And she would have to see that Reuben was kept away from him too. Old Hamish was mad enough to do anything: chop people up, shove them into acid baths. He was a menace. She knew she really ought to tell Mum and David what had happened this afternoon. But if she did, there would be an awful fuss, especially when David saw Hamish's red finger-marks on Lucy's neck and arm. David hated physical violence. He had complained to the Head of Lucy's last school because there was a teacher there who rapped the pupils over the knuckles with a ruler. As for Mum, if she discovered how Old Hamish had behaved, she would probably decide to move house again. And that was the last thing Lucy wanted. She would just have to invent some story about meeting Old Hamish staggering drunkenly along the path using terrible language. That would put the wind up Mum all right. She hated Reuben hearing bad language. She would certainly keep him away from Old Hamish if Lucy told her that.

8

The Poetry Competition

Lucy could hardly drag herself out of bed on Tuesday morning. She was exhausted. For half the night she had been dreaming that yellow gnomes were chasing her up and down dark stairways; the other half she had spent worrying about David and Mum and the insurance money.

Yesterday, when Lucy had seen what her mother had bought for their tea, she had thought it was a kind of celebration. She had naturally assumed that smoked salmon, fillet steak, chocolate mousse and after-dinner mints meant that David's relations had turned up trumps and lent him the thousand pounds. It was only afterwards, during their Mozart record concert (with Mum acting as disc-jockey), that Lucy had begun to suspect she had jumped to the wrong conclusion. For she had gradually noticed that David was not looking either happy or carefree, as he surely ought to be. On the contrary, he was sitting hunched up in his chair, staring fixedly ahead of him, and running his finger back and forwards over his moustache as he did when he was worried.

Lucy had cornered her mother in the kitchenette at supper-time and had asked her outright what had happened in Dundee. Sure enough Mrs

Bell had confessed that David's family had refused to give him a penny.

'Oh, Lucy! Use your imagination,' her mother had whispered. 'How do you think poor David must be feeling after being refused help by his own flesh and blood? This is when he needs his morale boosted. If they had given him the money, we could just have had eggs and spaghetti for tea.'

There was the same glassy stare in Mum's eyes that came when she opened the horrible buff-coloured envelope and saw how much the telephone bill was. On those occasions she usually rushed to the phone to make a long-distance call to her sister, Rose, whom she didn't even like. Lucy had once heard a phrase which she thought exactly described her mother in a crisis: 'Flying in the face of Fate.' That was what Mum tried to do. The trouble was, if you were her daughter, you had no option but to go along with her, even if you could see it was a kamikaze flight.

But this morning Lucy had a crisis of her own looming. The thought of it took away her appetite, so she set off for school feeling empty and queasy. The copy of the *Dream*, with its defaced and illegible page 12, felt like a lead weight in her bag.

Fiona Donald didn't help. All through R.I. she kept giving Lucy long, doleful looks which were about as comforting as reading her obituary notice to her. Lucy's sense of impending doom grew with every passing minute. By the time she sat down at her desk in Aggie's room, she felt beyond either hope or consolation. She just wanted what was going to happen to her to happen quickly.

Even this was to be denied her, though. For,

when Aggie sailed unsmilingly into the room, not only was she brandishing her copy of the *Dream*, but she had 3A's essay books in the crook of her arm. She banged these down on her desk, looked round the class, then rubbed her hands the way a butcher might before he starts attacking a carcase. Lucy groaned inwardly. They were obviously about to have their essays returned. She wondered if Daniel had been kept waiting like this before being thrown to the lions.

Aggie had obviously gone to town on the essays. Even Lucy in her distracted frame of mind soon noticed that all around her people were showing signs of shock, of being mortally offended. Fiona started sniffing when she saw what had been written in her book. And Alistair Scott, who thought himself the class intellectual, was giving subdued, but audible, gasps of outrage.

Aggie had her own idiosyncratic method of returning exercise books. Seated behind her desk, she would call out a name in a loud monotone, and when its owner approached within arm's reach, she thrust out the book without looking up. By ten fifteen she had given back twenty-five books and tossed two aside because their owners were absent. It suddenly dawned on Lucy that the one book still lying on the teacher's desk must be hers. But for some reason Aggie appeared to have suspended operations. Why hadn't she returned Lucy's book, too?

Lucy broke out into a cold sweat. She knew what was going to happen. Aggie was going to tear her essay apart in public. Some teachers enjoyed doing that. If a class had annoyed them, they picked out one victim to be the scapegoat. She was going to be savaged even before they

61

came to Oberon's speech. The dismembering of Lucy Bell was going to take the place of a commercial break between the essays and Shakespeare.

She was so tense that at first she could not comprehend what Aggie was saying as she rose from her chair and strode forward, waving Lucy's essay book at the class. She finally tuned in as Aggie said:

'So pay attention now, and you will hear what I expect in the way of a Third Form essay. This is a true story. Lucy Bell has written it simply and movingly, with none of the exaggerated sentimentalism which nauseated me in most of the others. Here it is, then. "My Hero", by Lucy Bell.'

Lucy's face was burning. She didn't know where to look. In the end she fixed her eyes on the photograph of Dylan Thomas that was pinned up on the wall to the right of the blackboard.

It was disturbing to hear her private thoughts being spoken aloud, especially in Aggie's posh voice. Lucy had never had an essay read out in class before. Teachers didn't do that sort of thing nowadays, Mr Walton said. They were all fanatically opposed to what they called competitiveness in the classroom. Mr Walton refused to grade their essays at all, even into As, Bs, and Cs. If he liked your work, he wrote 'Good' at the end of it, but in tiny letters, so that your neighbour wouldn't see it and get a complex.

Aggie obviously didn't care if Fiona got a complex. At the foot of Lucy's essay she had written 19/20 in giant figures. And beneath that, a big, bold, 'Excellent'. There was a p.s. in normal-sized writing. It said, 'See me in my room at four o'clock.'

It had all turned out so differently from what

Lucy had been expecting that she felt almost concussed. She even left her place after a moment and wandered over to show Aggie how she had accidentally ruined her copy of the *Dream*. Nor did she feel unduly astonished when the teacher observed mildly that that particular copy had been on its last legs anyway, and Lucy was to throw it in the bin and find another in the cupboard.

Her brain had resumed normal service by the end of the lesson, which was just as well since everyone came crowding around her to ask her questions about Marmion Bell and the fire, and to look at the scar on her head where the flames had caught her. Fiona went into a brief huff because she felt a best friend ought to have been told the story before . ('She never even told me her father was a *poet*,' Lucy heard her complain bitterly to Hazel Black.) But Fiona re-established contact as soon as she heard about Aggie's enigmatic 'p.s.'.

'*Lucy!* What can it *mean*? What can she want to *see* you for?' she asked at least half-a-dozen times during the day.

Lucy hadn't a clue. But she felt that the Fates were on her side today. So she wasn't nervous, only curious. At the end of her last lesson, she bypassed the cloakroom, ran along the corridor to Aggie's room, and tapped on the door.

'Come!' Aggie called. Her voice sounded different – slightly trilling, and more loosened up than it normally was.

Lucy saw why when she stepped inside. The Head was there, too, standing with his arms folded across his fat stomach, and with a big grin on his rosy face as though he and Aggie had been swapping jokes.

'Ha!' he cried, when he spotted Lucy. 'So

63

here's the clever wee lass! Mrs McLintock's been praising your work to the skies, my dearie.' The Head was always very Scottish and very jolly when he talked to you on your own.

Lucy was trying to work out what was different about Aggie. Suddenly she realized what it was. Aggie was smiling. She had the kind of smile that made her eyes turn narrow and almost vanish. She looked like a cat. And when she spoke she sounded like a cat, too, for she was almost purring.

'Ah, yes, Lucy! Come over here to my desk, dear. There's a wee matter the Head and I would like to discuss with you.' She held out a pale green slip of paper. 'Read this, Lucy. See what you think. Take your time. No hurry.'

Lucy looked down at the paper. It was headed: DAVID HOGG MEMORIAL POETRY COMPETITION FOR SCHOOLS.

Schools are asked to submit one entry for each age-group in the above competition, Lucy read. *The age-groups are a) 14 years and under, and b) 15-18 years.*

There will be two prizes awarded in each section. Each winner will receive £100, and their respective schools will receive £500 worth of books of their choice from Doyle and Anderson, Book-sellers, who are joint sponsors of this Award with the Teuchter Building Society.

Poems may be of any length and on any subject. Originality will be an asset. Their authenticity must be vouched for by the appended signatures of two teachers. Entries will be received up to and including the 15th of April.

'Well? What do you think, my bonnie lass? Can you do it? Can you help fill up the bare shelves in our library?' The Head tweaked Lucy's hair playfully. 'Mrs McLintock here has great hopes of you.'

Lucy was flabbergasted. Before she had gathered her wits together, the Head murmured confidentially, 'Mrs McLintock has been keeping her eyes open for some time for a likely entrant for Group A. It's the only way we can do it, things being as they are at the moment. Understaffing, you know. Working to rule. Union directives . . . But there! That's none of your concern, wee lass,' he finished, throwing back his shoulders and beaming at Lucy. 'All you have to do is write the winning poem, ho, ho!'

Lucy wasn't into writing poetry. Up until now, at any rate, she had been strictly a prose person. An essay, a piece of interpretation, a précis, any of these she would have tackled willingly. But a poem?

'I'm not sure that I can, Mr Ross,' she began nervously.

'Lucy, dear! I *know* you can,' Aggie cried. 'Otherwise I would never have suggested you. I was extremely impressed by that essay of yours. And the fact that your late father was a poet . . . It's obvious you have inherited his literary talent.'

'And you won't be on your own, lass,' the Head pointed out kindly. 'You and our other entrant are to get together once a fortnight and have a look at each other's progress. That was Mrs McLintock's idea. A kind of mutual therapy session like they have at her Writers' Circle. And *he* is an older man, Lucy. So you'll be able to cry on his shoulder if it all gets too much for you.' He winked and gave Lucy a nudge.

'I'm not sure,' Lucy was muttering again, when there was a sudden firm knock on the door.

'Ah! That will be him!' cried the Head. 'Our

Group B man. Come away in, Douglas!'

Douglas Gordon came striding in, smiling and self-assured, all blazer-braid and badges. He nodded politely to the Head and Aggie. Then he turned to Lucy.

'Hello, there! Are you to be my partner in crime?' he asked cheerfully.

Lucy gripped Aggie's desk to steady herself. The room had gone all misty, and she couldn't speak for the lump in her throat. But she managed to nod.

The Head gave a happy chuckle and rubbed his hands together.

'There you are!' he said, looking triumphantly at Aggie. 'It might be a wheen of years since I've taught them. But I haven't lost the knack of handling them. Pass that round the staffroom, Mrs McLintock!'

9

In Her Father's Footsteps

Lucy couldn't wait to tell Mum and David she had been chosen to represent Whitefields School in the poetry competition along with The Great Douglas Gordon. It was the best thing that had ever happened to her. She knew her mother had been disappointed when it became clear that Lucy would never play either the piano or the violin. Now Mum would see this was because Lucy was to follow in her father's footsteps. It was the hand of Fate.

Having told her news to Fiona and Hazel, who were waiting for her outside the school gate, she ran on ahead of them, and was scarlet-cheeked and breathless when she finally burst into the living-room. Then all the happiness drained out of her. For it was obvious that some fresh disaster had struck. Mum and David were sitting at the table wearing taut, tragic expressions. Reuben, his face all red and puffy with weeping, was on his mother's knee, one arm flung around her neck.

What had happened? Had one of their relatives died? Had Mr Tomney decided he couldn't wait for the thousand pounds? Was he going to have David sent to prison straightaway?

'What's wrong? What is it?' Lucy asked,

rushing forward. Her voice was squeaky with apprehension.

'Oh, darling!' Her mother leaned forward and squeezed Lucy's hand. 'We've just heard some terrible news. The Housing Company has sold the Big Green to the Corporation behind everyone's back. They're going to build flats on it.'

'The bulldozers are to move in tomorrow,' said David bitterly.

When he was angry his eyes seemed to turn a shade darker. Now, beneath his drawn brows, they looked almost navy-blue.

Lucy went limp with relief. 'Oh, gosh! Is that all? I thought it was something serious,' she exclaimed, sitting down heavily on the one unoccupied dining-chair.

David and her mother exchanged startled glances. Reuben's head shot round.

'Serious?' David repeated, as though unsure of what he had heard.

Mum stared hard at Lucy. 'You're obviously spending too much time with that Donald girl,' she said frostily. 'You're losing sight of what's important in life. You'll be wanting to chat about clothes and wallpaper next.'

Lucy's face burned. Her mother didn't often turn on her. But when she did, she could be really crushing.

'I . . . I didn't mean it wasn't serious,' she stammered. 'I just meant it might have been worse.'

'We're going to organize a petition. You can help to take the sheets round, Lucy,' David said quickly. He could never bear to watch anyone squirm.

'And if the partition doesn't work, Rufus'll blow their stupid houses down like the Big Bad

Wolf!' Reuben cried, wriggling down from his mother's knee and flinging his arms around his imaginary dog's neck.

'Poor Rufus! If they go ahead, he'll have nowhere to run,' Mrs Bell said, smiling sadly.

She looked as doleful as the Mona Lisa. Lucy decided she had better wait until later to tell her good news. Otherwise she was going to feel like someone cracking jokes at a funeral-tea.

'Lucy!' Mrs Bell gasped. She clapped her hands to her head. 'How could you! What has come over you?'

Lucy stared at her mother in astonishment. It was what had come over *her* that was worrying Lucy. Mum had been delighted at first when she had heard about the poetry competition. But now, in a matter of minutes, there had been this total transformation. It had happened when Lucy had given her her 'Hero' essay to read.

'You'll grow up to be one of those women who tells the passenger in the next seat all her family's private business between bus-stops,' Mrs Bell cried, thrusting the essay back at Lucy with a look of disgust.

To begin with, Lucy was so hurt she couldn't raise her eyes from the tablecloth. Then suddenly she was seething with anger.

'I see. Not a word about my getting nineteen out of twenty and an "Excellent". Yet you go into ecstasies about Reuben's daft songs. It's obvious who's the favourite in this house,' she shouted, biting her lip to stop her tears.

David, who had just put Reuben to bed, slipped past them into the kitchenette and began washing up noisily.

'You'll have to learn, Lucy Bell, that you don't

go round the world wearing your heart on your sleeve. If your heart's worth anything at all, that is,' her mother snapped.

'What you really mean is that you want to forget that Marmion Bell ever existed . . . in case you hurt your precious David's feelings. Isn't that it, Mum?' Lucy challenged, a tear escaping and running down her cheek. 'That's why we don't talk about him any more, isn't it? Well, I'm not going to forget him. He was my father. And if I want to tell people about him, you're not going to stop me, so there!'

She fled into the lobby and pulled her duffel-coat from the hallstand.

Her mother came running out after her. 'Lucy! Where are you going?' she said sharply. Her face had gone as white as paper.

'I'm going to the Donalds',' Lucy said, glaring at her. 'I love it round there. Fiona's mother keeps it so clean and tidy. It makes such a change.'

She flounced out and was halfway down the path when her mother's wavering voice called anxiously, 'Lucy! You will keep to the well-lit streets when you come home? Don't take any short cuts. And be back here by nine thirty at the latest.'

A lump rose in Lucy's throat. She felt like she had done on that terrible evening last summer when Reuben had been tormenting her and she had finally lost her temper and pushed him away. She had used so much force, he had fallen against the sharp corner of the sideboard and split his head open. To make it worse, when they had been stitching him up at the hospital, he had told them he had tripped over his dog. Not a word had he said to anyone outside the family about Lucy.

Mum could be just as irritating as Reuben at times. And she could really hurt Lucy's feelings, as she had done this evening. But Lucy knew that her mother loved and cared desperately about what happened to her. She shouldn't have said those cruel things to Mum about Marmion Bell, or insinuated that 10 Nevis Drive was dirty and uncomfortable. She paused, her hand on the gate. Should she go back now and make it up with her? After all, Fiona wasn't expecting her this evening.

As she hesitated, the door of number eight suddenly opened and Old Hamish emerged wearing his overcoat, cap and muffler. Lucy knew by the carrier bag he was clutching that he was bound for the pub. He jumped nervously when he saw Lucy in the dusk. Then he started down the steps as fast as his shaky legs would carry him.

'Hey! Lulu!' he croaked, flapping his hand to signal to her to stay put.

But Lucy was halfway down Nevis Drive before he had reached the gate.

10

Rory Speaks Out

There were no flats in Bunnyland. The houses were all semi-detached with two rooms on the ground floor and three bedrooms upstairs. The Donalds called the front room downstairs the 'lounge', and the back room the 'dinette'. The lounge was a kind of showroom. Lucy had never seen anyone actually sitting in it. But there was usually some new exhibit on display. As soon as Fiona had hung Lucy's coat in the cupboard, Mrs Donald would pop out from the kitchen, or come rattling down the stairs, calling excitedly, 'Lucy! Come through to the lounge and see what we've got!'

This evening they'd got a new tapestry-covered, three-piece suite, with matching curtains, and a tapestry-covered footrest in the shape of a pig. Lucy thought the pig, with its orange glass eyes and short, polished wooden legs, was nearly as repulsive as Old Hamish's gnome.

'Well? What do you think, Lucy?' Mrs Donald asked anxiously.

Ailsa, who had been in the middle of setting her mother's hair and was still hovering behind her with the rollers, said, 'We're worried about the carpet, Lucy. You don't think it clashes, do you?'

'It's the *wallpaper* that's bothering *me*,' sighed Fiona. 'It just doesn't look *right* any more. What do *you* think, Lucy?'

'What do you think about the *pig*, Lucy?' called a mocking, falsetto voice from the hall.

'Rory!' Fiona and Ailsa cried together in fury.

For once Lucy was grateful to Rory Donald for poking his nose in. For by the time Fiona and Ailsa had finished complaining about his being an embarrassment and a torment to them, they had all forgotten they were waiting for Lucy's opinion, and had gone back to the dinette.

There was a new piece of furniture in here, too, this evening.

'Look, Lucy! I got a bookcase out of my catalogue. That should be up your street. We've been hearing about your literary talents,' Mrs Donald called, as Ailsa shoved her under the dryer.

'What do you think, Lucy? Do you think it looks trendy? Mum let me have a free hand,' Fiona said, kneeling in front of the bookcase. She pointed proudly to the two green fans and the red cricket-ball she had arranged artistically on the bottom shelf, to the green alarm-clock and the red teapot on the middle shelf, and to the six books – three with green spines, three with red – on the top shelf.

'Great. Yes, it's lovely,' murmured Lucy politely. 'What books did you choose, Fiona?'

There was a snort from the corner where Rory was crouched over a chessboard. (He was barred from his room this evening, because Mr Donald was papering it.)

Fiona threw her brother a malevolent look. 'They're not real books, Lucy,' she explained. 'They're imitation. They sell them in the video shop. You're supposed to keep your cassettes in them.'

When Mrs Donald's hair was dry, she called her husband and they all had tea. It came rolling in on a new cane tea-trolley, teapot and crockery up above, fresh cream sponge, apple pie, and caramel wafers below.

'This is why we all die of heart-disease in the west of Scotland, eating food like this,' Rory informed them as he took the biggest piece of sponge.

'Here! Lay off, son!' cried Mr Donald, giving Lucy a cheerful wink. 'I'm getting to the vulnerable age. I don't like being reminded I'm not immortal.'

'Lucy's father died when she was only four months old,' Fiona observed in a melancholy voice. 'I think that was awful sad.'

Everyone looked uncomfortable. And from then on no one seemed to know quite what tone to take. Mr Donald, who was a naturally jolly man, made a few subdued little jokes. Mrs Donald burbled on quietly about nothing in particular. Lucy began to feel like the spectre at the feast. It came as a relief when the reproduction seventeenth-century Dutch wall-clock struck nine o'clock.

'Thanks for the supper, Mrs Donald,' she said, jumping up. 'I'll have to go. Mum'll worry if I'm late.'

Fiona brought Lucy's coat and helped her on with it. Then, as Lucy moved towards the door, Rory drank what was left of his tea and stood up.

'I'd better walk Lucy home,' he said casually. 'There are some pretty dark stretches between here and Nevis Drive.'

They all stared at him – his family with mistrust, Lucy with ill-concealed dismay.

'Are you serious, Rory?' Ailsa asked after a moment.

'Of course I am,' Rory said indignantly. 'What do you think? I'll just get my jacket, Lucy.' The next moment his feet hammered up the stairs.

Fiona and Ailsa collapsed on each other's shoulders, snivelling and snorting.

'Shut up, you two!' Mrs Donald hissed. But Lucy saw her own chin wobble as she and her husband exchanged glances.

Lucy hated the lot of them at that moment. She had a fifteen-minute walk ahead of her with Rory Donald. The prospect was appalling.

Rory started talking as soon as the gate had clicked shut behind them.

'I sometimes despair of my family, Lucy,' he said. He was taking long, slow strides, his eyes fixed on the ground. 'I mean, who else do you know who would buy an expensive new bookcase and fill it with ornaments and cassette cases? Somebody like you – from a background like yours – must think they're really stupid.'

Lucy was too taken aback to make any comment. But it didn't matter. Rory wasn't looking for responses. He just wanted to talk.

'I mean, don't think I'm not fond of them, Lucy,' he went on as they turned the corner. 'I am. That's what makes me sad for them. I really am sad. Their lives are so empty. Mum and the girls spend all their time thinking about clothes and hairstyles and furniture. And when Dad's not working, all he does is paper and paint and watch daft TV programmes. I can't interest them in anything worthwhile. It really frustrates me. That's why I sound so bitter and twisted sometimes.'

'That's just how my mother feels about her sister, Rose, and my Gran,' Lucy said thoughtfully. 'She says they have their priorities wrong. Mind you,' she added, 'from what I hear, they think she has her priorities wrong, too.'

'I knew you'd understand,' Rory said. 'That's why I made up my mind to speak out tonight. You see, I've always been so embarrassed for them in front of you – knowing that your mother was a musician and all that. Now I feel even worse, what with your father being a poet and you gifted that way yourself.'

'Oh, I don't know about that . . . ' Lucy said hastily.

Rory wasn't listening, though. He was still in full spate and flowing off now in another direction. 'Take this chess business,' he said. 'Well, I am keen on it. But not to the extent they think. Lucy, tell me this. When you're sitting with your family in the evening are there ever times when you don't talk to one another? When you just sit quietly and think?'

'Oh, yes,' said Lucy. 'That's a regular thing with us.'

It was true. Often, long silences fell in the living-room while all of them, even Reuben, sat staring into space.

'Well, in our house,' said Rory in a low, bitter voice, 'if anyone's quiet for even a couple of minutes, Mum thinks they're not feeling well. Or the girls think they've gone into a huff. Honestly, it's awful! Continuous chatter is the norm. That's why I often bring my chessboard downstairs and pretend I'm working out a problem. It's my only defence.'

Lucy, remembering how Fiona did rattle on at times, thought she would find it wearing too, contending with Fiona as well as two others.

'Never mind, Rory,' she said sympathetically. 'You'll soon be old enough to move into a bed-sit.'

'The way I feel at the moment, I'll move into a monastery where there will be no women and no talking, either,' Rory said with a sigh.

They looked at each other and laughed. Because they were between lampposts, Lucy couldn't see Rory's freckles. Without them he was quite good-looking, she decided.

They turned into Nevis Drive.

'Well, I've enjoyed our talk,' said Rory. 'It's done me good.'

They walked up the hill in companionable silence.

When they came to her gate, Rory put a hand on Lucy's shoulders. 'Good luck with the poem,' he said earnestly. 'And remember. Don't let The Great Douglas try to put you in the shade. He can be a bit overbearing at times. After all, his father's only a bank manager. Yours was a real poet.'

He turned and strode off down the hill, turning at the first lamppost to wave to her.

Lucy waved back. Rory Donald was all right, she decided. In fact he was quite good company. She shouldn't have believed all Fiona had said about him. She was smiling to herself as she started up the path, thinking about Rory going into a monastery. Then she gave a little cry of alarm. A figure had suddenly detached itself from the dark corner of the building and was coming unsteadily towards her.

'Hey, Lulu! You havnae told anyone? You havnae told, hen? Have ye?' Old Hamish was weaving his way along the path, bent on a collison course.

Lucy side-stepped him nimbly, yelled a vicious 'NO!' in his ear, and bolted for her own front door.

'Drunken old fool!' she muttered angrily. 'He should be locked away.' Once inside, she had to lean against the lobby wall until her heart had slowed down.

David had gone to see the chairman of the Tenants' Association about the Big Green petition, and Mrs Bell was sitting alone in the living-room, reading. As soon as she saw Lucy, she laid down her book and hurried over to give her a hug.

'Oh, I'm sorry I flew at you, pet,' she said in a voice full of remorse. 'I was still in a state of shock about the Big Green. I wasn't in control of myself.'

'But it was me writing about Marmion Bell that set you off, wasn't it?' said Lucy watching her closely. 'Why, Mum?'

Her mother made the kind of grimace Lucy had seen on her face when she was trying to convince herself she understood her income-tax form.

'Look! All I'm trying to do is teach you self-defence, darling,' she said in a weary voice. 'The more we tell other people about our private lives, the more vulnerable we are. I'm just trying to protect you, Lucy.'

Lucy was only just managing to hold back a yawn. She had had a hectic day, and quite suddenly she felt shattered. To be honest, she didn't have a clue what her mother was rambling on about. But she didn't think it mattered. What was important was that Mum had apologized for hurting her and wanted them to be friends again.

Lucy gave her a quick, hard hug, said goodnight, then staggered through to her bedroom. She could not even find the energy to wash herself before she slipped beneath her quilt. The thought flitted through her mind that she was getting as bad as dirty Old Hamish, but the next moment she was oblivious, breathing gently into her pillow.

11

'Death of an Onion'

Lucy had never dreamed it would be so difficult to write a poem. Each evening, after she had finished her homework, she sat cross-legged on her bed with her eyes shut, hoping for inspiration that never came.

'Wait for a thought or an idea that really moves you,' Aggie had told Lucy when she handed her the thick, A4-notebook that went with the assignment. 'Then just let yourself drift with the tide.'

By the end of a week, though, Lucy still had not left the shore. All she could show for her hours of meditation were a couple of lines, and four titles, three of which were now crossed out. The crossed-out titles were 'Violin Music', 'The Big Green', and 'Rain at Night'. Underneath 'Cat in the Rhubarb' she had written:

'His tail waves and his eyes gleam.
A bird is pecking near his hideout.'

When she re-read the two lines this evening, a look of disgust came over her face. The words had not sounded too bad when they were inside her head. But, written down, they looked like one of Reuben's daft songs. She picked up her pen and scored through them angrily. She certainly wasn't going to read that rubbish out to Douglas Gordon when they met on 22 February.

How on earth had her father written all those poems? A whole bookful of them! Maybe it was like learning to ride a bicycle, she thought. Once she had the knack there would be no stopping her.

'Just have patience, pet. Don't try to rush it,' was the only advice her mother had offered when Lucy had asked her if she could give her any tips.

Lucy felt that her mother wasn't as interested in the poetry competition as she ought to have been. She and David were too busy trying to organize a sit-in (or a 'sit-on' as Reuben called it, since it was to be *on* the Big Green) for 22 February, when the Corporation builders were due to start work. The house was like a fairground every evening with the telephone ringing continually and loyal supporters arriving to tear their hair and gnash their teeth over cups of tea.

Personally, Lucy was bored by the whole business. She reckoned the SOBG (Save Our Big Green) Action Group should bow to the inevitable, particularly now that the bulldozers had been in and transformed it from a Green, to a Brown. Mum and David didn't see it that way, though. They said the ground could be reseeded with wild grasses if they won, and made to look better than before.

What worried Lucy most of all was that her mother and David seemed to have forgotten for the moment about Mr Tomney and his thousand pounds. She felt they had pushed it to the back of their minds the way Mum shoved bills to the back of the bureau. They certainly were not talking any more about how they might raise the money. David had given up writing to friends and relatives who he thought might help him. For the moment he was his old cheerful self again, whistling happily as he designed eye-catching posters for the SOBG Campaign, or composed letters to send to the local paper.

Sometimes Lucy felt quite murderous towards David and her mother. They had no right to be so daft and irresponsible. She told herself she was sick to the teeth worrying about them, and that David could go to jail for all she cared. Nevertheless, she couldn't stop worrying – especially at nights when she was trying to fall asleep. No wonder she couldn't write her poem, she thought bitterly. She was handicapped. She lived in a crazy household where the children had to worry about the grown-ups instead of the other way about.

February 22nd turned out to be a disaster on all fronts. Only a dozen SOBG protesters turned up to challenge the squad of workmen who were starting operations on the Big Green. The workmen pretended that the protesters were invisible and stared through them. So very soon the protesters lost heart and began to trickle away. By ten o'clock only Mrs Bell and David were left, holding a placard that was falling to bits in the rain and bore what now looked like an inscription from a Roman temple:

AVE
O
REE

Mrs Bell was furious. She had lost a morning's teaching to make this demonstration, and had dirtied her Black Watch skirt on the muddy ground, all for nothing. She told David, as they set off for home, that in her opinion, Old Whitefields deserved to lose the Big Green, and that she hoped the flats would be an eyesore, and a breeding ground for vandals. David, tight-lipped, threw the placard down and stamped it into the mud.

Lucy's disillusionment came at the end of the day. It had been arranged that she and Douglas Gordon should meet in Aggie's room at four o'clock, and spend half an hour reading out any poems they had written, and exchanging ideas and opinions on them.

From three o'clock onwards she was like a cat on hot bricks. All through the music lesson she gazed out of the window, drumming her fingers on the desk and shuffling back and forwards on her seat until Fiona gave her an exasperated punch. Every time she thought of being alone with Douglas Gordon for half an hour her heart gave a great lurch. She still hadn't written a decent line of poetry. But she had a whole string of questions ready to ask The Great Douglas about his method of writing poems: how he found his ideas, how he decided on a metre, and so on. But a quarter of an hour after meeting Douglas it became quite obvious to Lucy that he wasn't interested in her struggles. All he wanted to do was stand behind Aggie's desk and listen to his own voice echoing in the empty classroom. He had written six poems in the past fortnight, all of them, in Lucy's opinion, distinctly peculiar, and most of them far too long. The oddest of the lot, 'Death of an Onion', seemed as pointless as it was long.

Once Douglas looked up at Lucy, flashed his famous smile, and said quietly, 'You'll notice the influence of Hamilton Finlay there.' And after his fourth poem, 'Computer at Prayer', he remarked complacently, 'Shades of Edwin Morgan . . . I hope.'

Lucy hadn't a clue who Douglas was talking

about. And what really annoyed her was that she felt Douglas knew this and was deliberately parading his superiority. She remembered what Rory had said about his being overbearing. It was true. The Great Douglas was on an ego trip. He just wanted Lucy to sit and look impressed.

By the time he got to the end of his last poem, 'The Drunken Osprey', their half-hour was up. He left her with a grin and a cheerful wave, but not a single word of encouragement. Lucy stared after him, feeling as though she had suddenly lost something she had treasured for a long time.

She walked home along Torridon Road in a wintry Glasgow drizzle that seemed to be seeping not only through her clothes, but through her skin as well. She felt let down and depressed. She passed the Big Green where cement-mixers whirled furiously and donkey-jacketed workmen squelched about in the mud. So much for the SOBG Action Group! She thought of all David's time and trouble, of all the cups of tea and telephone-calls her mother had made. She could have told them this would happen. She had known all along it was a fools' crusade.

As she trudged up the garden path, she caught a glimpse of Old Hamish's purply face and spiky hair at his bedroom window and hastily averted her eyes. Why couldn't they have a nice normal neighbour? Why couldn't they have a nice normal life? Rory Donald didn't know how lucky he was! All he had to worry about was his mother and sisters blethering on about furniture and clothes. She had the embarrassment of Mum and David not being married, the worry about David being sent to jail if they couldn't raise the thousand pounds, the aggravation of being pestered by a potty old drunkard who had a fixation about a gnome, as well as the daunting task of writing a poem, before mid-April, for the competition.

When she walked into the living-room she found David standing with his hands in his pockets staring moodily out of the window. Her mother, looking furious and red-faced, was mopping up milk from the carpet. And Reuben sat howling beneath the table because he'd just had his bottom smacked.

'Would you believe it?' Mrs Bell cried angrily to Lucy. 'We only had one jugful of milk left and he deliberately knocked it over.'

'Didn't!' wailed Reuben. 'Rufus did it. Told you so.'

It seemed that no one in the family had had a very good day.

12

Lucy to the Rescue

When Lucy got home from school at half past four on Monday, 9 March (one of her family's super-market days), she found a group of agitated-looking women standing on her path. They were gazing up at Old Hamish's kitchen window, out of which a tendril of smoke was floating.

Lucy's heart began to thump. She felt herself breaking out in a cold sweat as she always did when she had a shock.

'Here's the wee girl from the downstairs house,' a big-busted woman in a floral pinny called out. The others stopped looking at Ham-ish's window for a moment to stare at Lucy.

Hazel Black's granny, who lived at 5 Nevis Drive, came hurrying forward to grip Lucy's arm. 'Miss McCracken noticed the smoke about ten minutes ago,' she gasped excitedly. 'We've rung the bell and hammered on the door. But we cannae rouse him. God knows what's happened to the poor old devil! Mrs Burns has gone to phone for the fire brigade and the ambulance.'

'And never a man in sight when you need one, of course,' Miss McCracken, from number seven, cried angrily. 'A man could have been up that drainpipe and seen what was happening in there.'

'I could get up there,' said Lucy in a loud

voice. She had to speak loudly, because of the noise her heart was making banging in her ears.

The women stared at her, sizing her up.

'Are you sure, hen?' Granny Black asked dubiously. 'Have you ever done it before?'

'I went up Mrs McIver's drainpipe last summer when she locked herself out,' Lucy told her.

'Let her go up then,' rapped out Miss McCracken. 'I'd have done the same at her age. On you go, lass, and quickly!'

The women pushed Lucy through to the wall, and Granny Black and Miss McCracken gave her a leg up. It was an easy drainpipe to climb because there was a big fat ridge halfway up where the pipe from Lucy's house joined it. She found herself standing on Old Hamish's window-sill almost before she knew it, her left hand gripping the bottom rail of the small top window which was half open. She pressed her face against the larger pane and peered through the grimy glass.

Lucy gulped. What she could see inside was just like the illustration on the 'Electric Shock' page of the first aid manual she had been given at her last school. Old Hamish was lying face down on the floor, his right hand clamped over the plug of the iron which was plugged into the socket on the skirting board. The metal plate of the iron was slowly burning its way through the ironing board. That was where the smoke was coming from. There were no flames – at least, not yet.

'Can you see anything, hen?' the fat woman in the pinny called impatiently.

Lucy told them what she could see in a high, quavering voice. She was beginning to feel light-headed, and she was forced to grip the window-frame really hard, her hands were sweating so much. She would have to get back down to the ground quickly, she thought with a flutter of panic, otherwise she would fall.

Then something really strange happened. It was just as if someone had put a steadying hand on her shoulder. Lucy could almost feel the pressure of fingers, and a comforting sensation of someone friendly being close behind her, supporting her. She stopped feeling weak and trembly. Her head cleared. She listened for a moment for the ambulance, but, hearing no siren, she began to move carefully along the ledge to a point where she could reach down inside the window and unfasten the catch of the casement.

An 'Oh!' of alarm floated up to her from below.

'It's all right,' she called down. 'I'll go in and turn the power off and see how the old man is. Then I'll open the door to you.'

The window opened inwards. Lucy pushed it back against the wall and dropped lightly on to the kitchen floor. She blessed the social studies teacher at Westbank who had given them all those written first aid tests, which Lucy had moaned about at the time.

'Electrocution: Rule One. Never touch the casualty while he/she is still in contact with the electricity or you will be electrocuted yourself. Switch off the power. Or knock the casualty clear with something dry and non-conducting.' She knew it by heart still. A good thing, too!

She skirted the smouldering ironing-board, holding her hand over her face so she wouldn't inhale any fumes. She wasn't going to touch the iron; she wasn't going to touch anything until the power was off.

Stepping over Old Hamish, she ran across to the cupboard where the junction-box was housed and pushed the big lever to the 'off' position, then staggered back against the wall, breathing heavily. Her knees were beginning to wobble again. She was feeling sick. She hoped she wasn't going to have an attack of migraine.

'Come on, Lucy! Don't give up now,' a voice inside her head said urgently.

But was it inside her head? Suddenly she had the same feeling she had had on the window-sill; of someone strong and protective standing very close. But this time she found herself thinking, quite matter-of-factly, I know who it is. It's Marmion Bell come to help me. Her legs felt strong again. She was no longer sick. She could cope.

She ran back into the kitchen, filled the washing-up bowl with cold water and doused the smoking board. Then she took a deep breath. Now came the grim part. She had to see if Old Hamish were alive or . . .

She dropped on her knees beside him, her heart beating wildly and turned his head to one side. She could see that his face was a horrible grey colour. But when she put her own cheek close to it, she could just feel his breath. Lucy groaned with relief. The old man was unconscious. But he was still alive.

Gritting her teeth, she prised his fingers from the plug which fell with a clatter to the floor. His hand was still wet. He must have gone straight from the sink to the socket and given himself a massive shock.

Her stomach heaved as she smelled scorched flesh and saw the raw pulp that had been Old Hamish's palm. She had to keep her eyes averted from it as she struggled to pull his log-like body into the recovery-position, lying on his right side, with right arm and leg stretched out behind, and left arm and leg bent in front. When she had made sure his nose and mouth were clear of the floor, she took off her duffel coat and covered him with it.

As she straightened she heard the sirens, at first faintly in the distance, then gradually growing louder. She ran through the living-room, along the lobby and down the stairs to unlock the front door.

Mrs Burns had phoned for everything – police, fire brigade and ambulance. And they had all arrived at once. The old women stood in a huddle by the side of the path, watching the uniformed men clatter up Hamish's stairs behind Lucy.

When she had answered the men's questions, Lucy left them and went to sit on the window-sill in the living-room, hugging herself and trembling, not with cold, but with delayed shock. The firemen went away almost immediately, having checked that the electrical system was safe. Then Old Hamish was carried out, still unconscious, on a stretcher. Lucy had to look away quickly in case she started to cry. She had no great love for Old Hamish, but she always hated seeing people on stretchers. They looked so sad and helpless.

A big policeman with a black moustache came out of the kitchen and handed Lucy her coat. He patted her on the shoulder. 'You're a clever lass,' he said approvingly. 'You did all the right things. Tell your mum and dad they should be proud of you.'

Well, she needn't tell her dad, thought Lucy! She felt a cold prickling on the back of her neck. Up until now she had never believed in ghosts. But she had to believe the evidence of her own senses. Not that it had been a ghost, exactly, that

had turned up to help her. It had been more of a
. . . *presence*? Yes, that was probably the best
word to describe it.

As it turned out, her mother didn't need to be
told, either. For when Lucy and the policeman
left number eight a few minutes later, they found
Mrs Bell, David and Reuben standing on the path
open-mouthed, their shopping at their feet, while
the old women vied with one another to tell them
what had happened in their absence.

'Here she is now!' Granny Black cried suddenly, noticing Lucy on Hamish's steps. 'Give her
three cheers! Three cheers for the plucky wee
lassie!'

To hide her embarrassment, Lucy pushed
back her sleeve and looked down at her watch.
She couldn't believe it, when she saw the time. It
was only five o'clock. Was it only half an hour,
then, since she'd walked through that gate and
seen the smoke? It seemed to her like half a
lifetime ago.

13

Heroine

Lucy was given three cheers again next morning in the school hall. The jungle telegraph had been at work. It seemed that the whole of Toytown and Bunnyland had heard about Old Hamish's accident and how Lucy had gone to his assistance. The Head, who had called a special assembly in Lucy's honour, seemed to think she had shinned up the drainpipe mainly for the glorification of Whitefields Comprehensive, and to show certain snobby, fee-paying schools that, despite the University Bursary results, it was in the comprehensives that Scottish backbone and initiative were still to be found. That was the general tenor of his speech, anyway.

Aggie, congratulating Lucy privately after the English lesson, said that her brave action showed how strong were the forces of heredity, and that Marmion Bell's cape had obviously fallen on Lucy's shoulders in more ways than one. As Lucy was sidling in embarrassment to the door, Aggie, wearing her cat-smile, called after her.

'By the way! Any luck with the poem yet, Lucy?' she asked.

It was almost comic, the way the smile vanished when Lucy said, 'No.'

Lucy appreciated how Aggie must be feeling,

however. Three weeks had gone by and she still hadn't come up with a single poem. Poor old Aggie must be worrying that, after all her confident talk to the Head, she had backed a loser in Lucy Bell.

Lucy no longer spent her breaks with Fiona and Hazel gazing at The Great Douglas. Having suffered another of his tedious poetry-readings last week, she was now completely disenchanted with him. She had taken instead to strolling round the playground with Rory Donald, while she ate an apple and drank her Slimway lemonade.

Fiona thought this was very peculiar – even stranger than Lucy losing interest in Douglas Gordon.

'But do you not find Rory dead *boring*?' she had asked Lucy, her brown eyes popping. 'I mean, he's so *quiet* – unless he's being rude, that is.'

'He's not quiet with me,' Lucy had told her. 'He talks all the time. He's quite good company.'

'He *talks*? Our Rory actually *talks*?' Fiona had asked with an incredulous hoot. 'My goodness! At this rate, pigs'll be wearing kilts soon.'

Today, at break, Rory and Lucy were standing beside the playground railings discussing the pros and cons of the new flats which could already be seen, rising in the distance.

'It's who has the biggest claim, Lucy. Today's homeless. Or the future generations who cannot live by bread alone. That's how I see it anyway. Do you agree?'

Before Lucy could give an opinion, Alistair Scott came panting up to them, eyes gleaming excitedly behind his spectacles.

'Hey, Lucy!' he gasped. 'There's a reporter and a photographer from *The Graphic* waiting for you in the Head's office. You've to go over there at once. You're getting famous.'

'From the newspaper!' gulped Lucy. 'Oh, gosh.' Her face went scarlet, and she felt butterflies fluttering in her stomach.

'My, my! Now I wonder who could have telephoned the press!' Rory said with an ironic smile. He patted Lucy on the shoulders. 'On you go,' he told her cheerfully. 'Go and tell your story – for the greater glory of the school and you-know-who!'

'Not only the glory of the school,' said Alistair earnestly as he accompanied Lucy across the playground to the main building. 'The glory of 3A, too. No one from our form has ever been in the papers before. So don't hide your light under a bushel, Lucy.'

In fact, as Lucy found out when she walked into the Head's office, she wasn't going to have to say much at all. Mr Ross seemed bent on doing all the talking. (He and Douglas Gordon had a lot in common, Lucy thought.) Occasionally, the reporter (a blond, rosy-cheeked boy who looked no older than Rory) would interrupt the Head's narrative to ask Lucy how she had felt. And she would stammer out inanities like, 'Oh . . . f-frightened, I think you could say,' or 'Well, oh, determined, I suppose.' Meanwhile, the surly-looking elderly photographer shoved her head from side to side, or pushed her against the bookcase, or sat her on the Head's swivel chair, reading a copy of last year's school magazine.

Fortunately the newspaper reporters had left when the Head suddenly remembered that he had not mentioned one colourful aspect of Lucy's character.

'Damnation!' he cried, bringing his fist down

94

on the desk. 'I never told them you wrote poetry, and that we had entered you for the competition. That would do the school's image no end of good, too. Maybe I can still catch them.'

He shot out of the room and went pounding along the corridor suprisingly fast for a man with such short, fat legs.

When he returned, his face was crestfallen. 'Gone! Too late. Never mind,' he gasped, mopping his brow as he collapsed into his chair.

Lucy was immensely relieved. Bad enough that the Head, Aggie and The Great Douglas were all waiting for her to produce a prize-winning poem. If the readership of *The Graphic* had joined them she would have ended up with a nervous breakdown.

14

A Terrifying Experience

'Old Hamish has been asking to see you. He's evidently got a chest infection now, and his heart's a bit dicky. The ward sister has just phoned from the hospital,' Mrs Bell told Lucy when she came in from school on Wednesday afternoon.

'Oh, no! Will I have to go there tonight?' Lucy asked in dismay. She had a lot of homework. Besides, the very smell of a hospital made her nervous.

'That's entirely up to you,' said her mother coldly as she sailed back into the kitchenette.

Lucy glared at her, then marched through to her room, slamming the door shut behind her. She was getting really fed up with her mother nowadays. She was growing more unreasonable by the minute. At the moment she was in a huff because Lucy's story and photograph had appeared on page 2 of *The Graphic* this morning – something that would have delighted any normal mother. Even Aggie – when she had seen what a good photograph it was of Lucy sitting in the Head's chair – had sent a boy out to the news-agent's to buy her a copy. Yet Mum . . .

Lucy climbed up on to her bed and lay flat, staring at the ceiling and blinking back her tears.

What on earth was wrong with Mum? It had started last night, as soon as Lucy had announced she'd been interviewed by the press. Mrs Bell had looked just like the woman who gave the mime and movement lessons at the drama workshop last term. She had stood frozen in the kitchenette doorway, the soup tureen in her hands, not saying a word, but with her face registering 1) shock, 2) dismay and 3) disgust – in that order. Lucy had felt as though she'd just confessed to mugging Granny Black.

And David hadn't been much better. No, 'Fantastic, Lucy!' or, 'Great stuff, girl!' Just a mumbled, 'Well, it's done now, Laura. No point in getting het up about it,' to Lucy's mother.

Reuben was the only one who had reacted normally. Well, normally at least for Reuben, that was. The sight of Lucy's face staring up at him from the newspaper had sent him running round and round the living-room like a mad puppy. But at least he had cared enough to want to take the paper to school with him to show Lucy's photo to his teacher.

The truth of the matter was that her mother was a rotten snob, Lucy thought sourly. Not the sort of snob who looks down on people for being poor. But the kind who thinks it's bad taste to want to appear on television or to allow your good deeds to be written about in the news-papers. The way Mum saw it, Lucy had let the side down by telling the readers of *The Graphic* what a brave, clever kid she was. 'Plucky, viv-acious teenager' they had called her.

Well, let her mother think what she liked! Lucy had enjoyed her little bit of publicity. She had enjoyed being stopped by people in the school corridors who wanted to tell her how much they liked her photo. She leaned down and fished her own copy of *The Graphic*, which she had bought on her way to school, from her bag and opened it at page 2. Yes, it was a good photograph. Much better than any she had had taken in recent years. She might order a print of it from the newspaper office. Rory had said, flatteringly, that he was going to order one.

'Teenager's Courageous Rescue Bid' it said beneath the picture. She could have recited the paragraph that followed by heart, she had read it so many times.

Marmion Bell would have been proud of her too, Lucy thought, as she folded the paper carefully and shoved it beneath her pillow. He wouldn't have been a prig like Mum or a wet blanket like David.

And, come to think of it, that was something else Mum had tried to spoil for her. Last night, while David was in the bathroom, Lucy had started to tell her mother about the uncanny sensation she had experienced on Hamish's window-sill, and how she was convinced Marmion Bell had helped her. Mum had cut her short.

'Look. You did a very brave thing, Lucy,' she had said snappily. 'We all appreciate it. But there's no need to fantasize.'

Lucy had been so taken aback, she had just clammed up and gone off to her room. It was several minutes before the full meaning of what her mother had said dawned on her. Mum had actually accused her of lying!

She would have flown back into the living-room there and then and made a scene, but David had come in. And she hadn't felt like talking about Marmion in front of David. In fact, all the time Lucy had known David he had never once spoken to her about her father. She thought she knew why. Marmion Bell had been a very special person, a hero and a poet. David was quite ordinary. So, naturally, he was jealous, even of Marmion's memory. As for Mum, now that she had David, her dead husband's memory was just an embarrassment to her. Mum did not want to hear about Marmion Bell any more, Lucy thought bitterly.

It took Lucy half an hour to get to the hospital. She had a ten-minute wait at the bus-stop in Torridon Road, a ten-minute ride, and a ten-minute cold, wet walk at the other end. She still hadn't forgiven Old Hamish for the way he had manhandled her on his staircase. So, as she trudged along the corridors of the big, gloomy Victorian building looking for Ward M6, she wasn't feeling particularly like a ministering angel.

When she saw the old man, however, she had a shock. He seemed to have both aged and shrunk in two days. In fact, had it not been for the big white bandage on his burned hand, she might not have recognized him. He was in the bed nearest the door, propped up on two pillows, and gulping in air as though it were whisky.

He still had plenty of strength in his left hand, though. Lucy found this out as soon as she sat down by his bed and felt his fingers clamp round her wrist. He still had his surly temper, as well.

'What d'you mean by telling that reporter I was eighty?' he asked her straightaway. 'I'm not even seventy-eight till April!'

Then he had a fit of what sounded like whooping cough. Lucy thought he would never catch his breath.

'He does that all night. I cannae sleep for him,' a fat bald man in the next bed complained when Old Hamish's coughing had finally subsided.

Old Hamish threw him a vindictive look. Then he squeezed Lucy's wrist.

'Listen, hen,' he said hoarsely. 'I want you to do me a favour. Do you remember yon wee chessman of mine? The one your Reuben pinched?'

'Chessman?' said Lucy puzzled. 'Do you mean the wee yellow gnome?'

'Aye,' said Hamish crossly. 'My mannikin. But keep your voice down, will you? The whole ward will hear you.'

He let go of Lucy's wrist and lay back against his pillow to recover his breath. Then he pointed to his locker. 'Open that, Lulu,' he said. 'You'll see my front-door key. I want you to take it. When you get back home, run up to my bedroom. You'll find yon wee chessman sitting on top of my wardrobe, wrapped in a blue duster. Bring it here to me tomorrow. And no a word to a soul about it, mind!'

'But why do you want me to bring it here? You'll be coming home soon,' Lucy pointed out.

Hamish looked as murderous as was possible in view of his state of health. 'Don't argue, lassie!' he croaked. 'I have my reasons. Yon wee chessman happens to be my insurance for my declining years. I've hung on to it for fifty years. An' now I reckon it's safe to dispose of it. So I'm no runnin' the risk of havin' it stolen. Aye, an' there's plenty of folk would just love to get their hands on it, too,' he growled. 'So the sooner you bring it here, the happier I'll be. All right?'

As he went into another whooping-fit of coughs, the fat man in the next bed caught Lucy's eye and tapped his finger meaningly on his forehead. 'Pot-ty!' he mouthed.

A pang shot through Lucy as she watched Hamish's old body shaking and shuddering on the bed. It must be terrible to be weak and sick, she thought, with your poor old head full of strange fancies, and people like Fatty over there sneering at you. Why shouldn't she humour the old fellow?

She scowled at Fatty, and opened Old Hamish's locker. The key was lying on the top shelf. She took it and held it up so that Old Hamish could see it.

'Don't worry. I'll get you what you want, Mr Henderson. I'll bring it tomorrow,' she said loudly.

Old Hamish nodded. He looked like Methuselah with his parchment-skin and his faded old eyes. Yet once he must have been a strong, blue-eyed sailor.

As Lucy rose to leave, Old Hamish gave her an odd little smile.

'Hey, Lulu,' he gasped. 'Remember. If anything happens to me, that wee chessman's yours. You're the only lassie that ever put herself out to do me a good turn.'

Lucy waited uncertainly for a moment. But the old man had closed his eyes and seemed to have fallen asleep.

As Lucy came out into the corridor, a black nurse was reading the riot act to a small, thin bearded man who was hastily stubbing a cigarette out with his heel.

'Smoking outside the chest-and-heart wards! Heavens above! Have you visitors no sense! If

101

you don't care about your own health, you might consider our patients,' she ranted.

The man was saying he was sorry – very sorry. He hadn't been thinking. In between apologies he kept clearing his throat.

Lucy could hear his footsteps and his short dry cough as he followed her along the corridor and down two flights of stairs. The nurse must have frightened him away, she thought. It was still only halfway through visiting-time. Most visitors waited till the end. She heard the cough again as she walked out through the main gates of the hospital, past the porter's lodge.

It was still daylight, but the long road, swept by wind and rain, was deserted. As Lucy hurried along towards her bus-stop, with her head down, she could hear the quick, light step of the bearded man, and an occasional cough, behind her. She thought nothing of this at first. But then she had to stop to refasten the button of her duffel coat hood. The footsteps seemed to falter. Then they stopped as well. When Lucy started walking again, so did the bearded man. She quickened her pace. So did he.

Lucy gulped. She had once read in a magazine that you should never look round if you think someone is following you. It's bad psychology. It winds the pursuer up. So she walked on steadily, keeping her eyes fixed always on a spot some distance ahead. Then, to her horror, she remembered that she was coming to a particularly lonely stretch of road, with the cemetery on one side and a piece of waste ground on the other. Was the bearded man holding back until they reached it? Was he going to pounce on her there? Slap, slap, slap, went his shoes on the wet pavement behind her. Bang, bang, bang, went Lucy's heart. She turned weak and breathless with fear.

Suddenly she saw a narrow side road on the right. There were houses along it with gardens and hedges. If she could make it round the corner and dodge into a garden before the man saw where she had gone . . .

Lucy broke into a run, willing the strength back into her wobbly legs. She didn't know if the man had started to run too. She could hear nothing but her own heart banging madly in her ears. As she neared the corner she put on a tremendous spurt, then ran diagonally across the side street and through the gateway of a semi-detached house, whose small front lawn was bounded by a six-foot-high privet hedge.

She cowered behind the dripping hedge, shaking and gasping, praying that no one in the house would look out of a front window and see her. Her luck held. No one spotted her. And a few seconds later she heard feet running past on the pavement. She had been right, then! The bearded man had been after her.

When she judged it safe, she crept back along the path and out on to the pavement. Yes. There he was, almost at the end of the block – hurrying along the road, his head turning this way and that as he looked for her.

Lucy tore off, round the corner, and along past the cemetery and the waste ground to the bus-stop. Five minutes later she was sitting on the bus, weak with relief. It was her first experience of this kind of trouble. She supposed she had been lucky up until now. By fourteen you should more or less be able to look after yourself. She was almost at the end of her journey, however, before her heart was beating normally again. Then a woman behind her coughed suddenly, causing Lucy nearly to jump out of her skin. Being followed for five minutes had turned her into a nervous wreck. What would Mum say, she wondered, when she told her what had happened to her. Perhaps she wouldn't let her go down to the hospital again on her own.

As it turned out, though, she never got round to telling her mother about the sinister man who had followed her. When she walked into the living-room she found a scene of deepest gloom. David was sitting at the table, pen in hand, staring at an advert in *The Graphic* which was headed, 'Do You Need Money Fast? Borrow From Us!', while her mum was slouched on the piano-stool slowly playing something melancholy by Debussy. It suddenly dawned on Lucy that March was halfway gone. They were hurtling towards April. Time was running out fast – for everyone.

15

Too Late

The hospital visiting-hour was from three to four o'clock on Thursday so Lucy had to ask for an exeat from school. The Head was delighted for her to play ministering angel, now that she had finished with being a heroine. His only stipulation was that she should wear her school uniform.

After her frightening experience the night before, she was glad to find a whole procession of visitors making their way up the long, straight road to the hospital. It presented a totally different aspect today with the sun shining and a brisk north-westerly wind whisking chip-papers and lolly-wrappers out of the waste ground and over the railings into the cemetery. The bearded stranger began to seem very unreal. She could almost have imagined he had been part of a bad dream.

Lucy had had to pretend to her mother and David that Old Hamish had asked her to bring him something – anything – to remind him of home. She had come back down from his flat holding a framed photograph of the Coorie Doon pub, which had been Old Hamish's favourite local until it was demolished. The gnome was in her pocket.

She patted it as she hurried along with the crowd. Old Hamish certainly had a fixation about it. It seemed it was a 'chessman' now. If it was, it was the queerest looking one she had ever seen. He seemed to think someone might want to buy it, too. That was absurd. Who would want to buy one solitary chessman?

But old people, living on their own, did get peculiar obsessions, she reflected. Look at Gran Campbell! She was convinced that her soapstone Buddhas looked unhappy unless she placed them facing a window. And Hamish wasn't just old and lonely. He was very often drunk as well. It wasn't surprising that his obsession had got such a hold on him.

Lucy found she couldn't like Old Hamish any better just because he had nearly electrocuted himself. How could she like someone who had deliberately frightened her out of her wits and given her nightmares? She would still give him a wide berth when he came home again. But she could feel sorry for him, for the time being, when he was lying in hospital looking helpless and pathetic. That was why she had decided to humour him and to take him his precious gnome. She would pretend she believed his stories about it, the way Mum pretended to believe in Reuben's motor-racing.

She strode into Ward M6, grinning cheerfully, only to discover that Old Hamish was nowhere to be seen. His bed was empty. Hamish's fat neighbour had obviously been looking out for the old man's visitor, for, as soon as he spotted Lucy, he stopped talking to his wife.

'Here! The old chap's been taken into Intensive Care. He took a bad turn about an hour ago.

You should go to Sister's office and find out what the score is,' he called out.

Lucy had no intention of doing anything of the sort. The very words 'Intensive Care' made her backbone prickle. If she went to Sister's office, Sister might expect her to go and look at Old Hamish lying with tubes sticking out of him and one of those bleepers beside him to monitor his heartbeat. Her head began to swim at the very idea. She was going to go home. Her mother could telephone the hospital and find out how Old Hamish was.

Lucy just missed a bus, finally catching the three-forty. It passed Whitefields Comprehensive at ten minutes to four, and she pressed her nose against the window, vainly trying to see into the first-floor art room where 3A would be 'tidying away' for Miss Gillies. Then her eye fell on a figure leaning against the brick pillar by the school gate and her heart gave a sickening jolt. It was the bearded man. She could swear to it.

The bus swung round the bend, past what had once been the Big Green and was now a building-site, and the school was lost to view. Lucy scrambled down the stairs on trembling legs and almost fell off the bus at the corner of Nevis Drive. She was shaking all over. Questions tumbled round and round her brain. Had it really been the man who had followed her? Or had it just been a waiting parent who happened to be small and thin and bearded? Had last night's frightening experience made her imagine things? Should she tell Mum her fears?

She found her mother sitting at the table cradling a cup of tea in her hands and staring bleakly out into the garden where Reuben was playing on his tricycle. When Lucy called her name, she jumped and turned round. Her face, Lucy saw to her dismay, was white and streaked with tears.

'What is it? What's happened now?' she asked tersely, her thoughts leaping, as they always did nowadays, to David and his problems.

'Oh, pet,' her mother said brokenly. 'It's so sad. Poor Old Hamish died forty minutes ago. You were probably at the hospital when it happened. They've just phoned to see if we had his door-key. The Social Services people will have to clear out his house . . . Och, and David and I were going to go up and make everything spick and span for his home-coming. Why do we always leave it too late to show folk we care about them?' she asked.

Lucy drew her breath in sharply as someone walked across the floor upstairs. It sounded just like Old Hamish.

'It's David,' her mother said quickly. 'He thought he would try to tidy the place up.'

They heard David's feet running downstairs. A minute later he walked in and dumped two carrier-bags, full of empty whisky-bottles, on the floor. 'There are plenty more where those came from,' he said with a sigh. 'I'm going to clear them all out, Laura. Why should strangers learn about the old chap's weakness?'

'It was probably the drink that really killed him,' said Lucy, swallowing hard. 'Why did he have to drink like that?'

David was frowning down at the bottles. 'He couldn't face up to life, Lucy,' he said. 'That's the short answer. My father once accused me of the same thing. He said it was the eighth deadly sin.'

108

'No! That's not true,' cried Mrs Bell in such a ringing tone, that both Lucy and David stared at her.

'Not true,' she repeated in a murmur as she picked up the carrier-bags and hurried out to the dustbin with them.

16

Rory Spots a Treasure

'Rory. Do you ever think about death?'

'I do when it happens to someone I know. It's only to be expected,' Rory said, matter-of-factly.

Lucy was glad that Rory hadn't laughed at her, or, even worse, been embarrassed by her raising such a morbid subject. She had been feeling so depressed since hearing about Old Hamish yesterday that she felt she must talk to someone about it.

'Dad was with our Grandpa when he died. And he said it was very peaceful. Just like a clock stopping. Not frightening at all. Does that help?' he asked kindly.

They were spending the second half of their dinner-break huddled with a crowd of others inside the bicycle shed, sheltering from a cutting north wind.

'What about life after death?' Lucy asked abruptly.

'Oh, well, I'm very open-minded about that,' Rory said, folding his arms and gazing thoughtfully across the playground. 'I have a feeling there's a lot going on in the universe that we haven't even begun to understand.'

'You see, I can't believe Old Hamish has been

snuffed out just like that,' Lucy burst out. 'Not because I like him particularly. But because . . . oh, I don't know! It doesn't seem fair. That's all. He was an old man. But he still had his dreams. He was still planning for the future. Look!'

She put her hand in her pocket and drew out the gnome, wrapped in its duster. 'I was to have taken this to him yesterday, Rory. He had some potty notion he could sell it for a lot of money. It was a kind of obsession with him. He said that I had to have it, if . . . ' Her throat tightened and her eyes began to smart. Who would ever have thought Old Hamish's death would have affected her like this?

She unwrapped the gnome and held it up so that Rory could see it. 'He said it was a chessman,' she said in a wobbly voice. 'I bet you've never seen a chessman that looked like that. I don't know how he got that idea in his funny old head.'

Rory gulped, then took the gnome from Lucy and stood staring down at it. His mouth opened and closed silently. He looked like a goldfish.

'What on earth's up with you?' said Lucy rudely. Her nerves were really on edge today. She couldn't stand Rory behaving strangely. He was usually so calm and dependable.

At first he didn't answer her. He stood shaking his head slowly from side to side. Lucy noticed that his freckles had almost disappeared, his face had grown so red. When he did finally find his voice it was hoarse with excitement.

'Lucy,' he said, staring at her, 'have you ever heard of the Lewis Chessmen? They're famous. Most of them are in the British Museum. The rest are here in Scotland.'

'No,' said Lucy. Her own heart was beginning to beat fast now, and she was feeling shivery with suspense though she didn't know why.

Rory handed the gnome back to her. 'Come on,' he said. 'There's a book in the library I want you to see. *Scotland's Treasures*, it's called. I was looking at it just the other day.'

He set off at a run across the playground with Lucy following. Fiona and Hazel, who were on their way to view The Great Douglas from afar, saw Lucy, and came running over to hand her their bags, so she could dump them in their form room. By the time Lucy had done this and joined Rory in the library, he was sitting at a corner-table with *Scotland's Treasures* lying open in front of him.

If anything, he was looking even more excited by now – quite goggle-eyed, in fact. There were a couple of sixth-formers working at another table, so he couldn't yell to Lucy. He had to be content with making faces and tapping a finger on the coloured photograph he had been studying.

Lucy took one look, then gasped and sat down heavily on the chair next to Rory's. The photograph was of a whole line of gnomes, close relatives to Old Hamish's from what she could see. The caption beneath them read:

'The fourteen knights from the twelfth-century Lewis Chessmen hoard, which was found in Uig Bay in 1831. There were ninety-three pieces in all, made of walrus-ivory. It is thought that one knight, four rooks, and forty-five pawns are still missing.'

Lucy set Old Hamish's gnome down on the glossy page. It was shiny with sweat from her palm.

'He's the fifteenth knight. Is that what you're thinking, Rory?' she asked in a shaky whisper.

Rory nodded slowly.

'Oh, gosh!' Bubbles of hysterical laughter rose in Lucy's chest. Had she really been carrying one of Scotland's treasures around in her pocket for two days, wrapped in a blue duster? She began to wheeze and splutter. The sixth-formers turned to glare at her.

Rory closed the book and stood up. 'Come on,' he whispered, nodding towards the door.

As soon as they were out in the corridor he turned to her.

'Where did the old man find it, Lucy?' he asked her eagerly. 'Did he tell you? Did he buy it somewhere?' He was cradling the gnome in his hand, stroking it gently with his forefinger.

Lucy leaned back against the wall, trying to remember. She didn't know what was wrong with her today. Now, all of a sudden, she felt close to tears. She had to swallow several times before she could speak. 'The last time I saw him – in hospital – he said something about how he had held on to it for fifty years . . . and now it would be safe to dispose of it . . . and that there were still people who would like to get their hands on it. I thought he was raving.'

'Do you think he st . . . came by it dishonestly?' asked Rory hesitantly.

Lucy had a sudden vivid memory of Hamish's villainous old face. Her eyes filled with tears. 'Yes. Very likely,' she said thickly.

'Still . . . that book we were looking at, it was only published last year,' Rory pointed out. 'And obviously no one knew then that a fifteenth knight had ever turned up. So it can't be officially

113

listed as stolen property, no matter how the old man got it.'

'No,' Lucy agreed dully.

'What I'm saying is, it must be rightfully yours, Lucy. To do what you want with it. To sell, if you like.'

Lucy stared at Rory blankly. Her brain seemed to have gone on strike.

'But who would I sell it to?' she asked.

'The British Museum!' Rory cried. 'They buy things from people all the time. They'll offer you a fortune for that. Four figures at least.'

'Four figures? A thousand pounds?'

'More. I'm sure they would.'

Lucy's heart gave a lurch. A thousand pounds! It would save David. Even if the money hadn't come through by April, Mr Tomney wouldn't prosecute if they could assure him it was on its way.

'Where will I send it to?' she asked in a shaky voice.

'I don't know exactly,' Rory told her. 'But I'll be seeing someone this evening who can tell me. Professor Livingstone. He's a member of our chess club. I'll sound him out about where to send finds. I won't tell him why I want to know. Don't tell anyone, either – apart from your family, of course. It might be risky.'

'I won't even tell them,' said Lucy. Her mother and David were still trying desperately to raise the thousand pounds. Tomorrow they were going down to Gran Campbell's after Old Hamish's funeral to see if she could help them. If Lucy told them about the chessman, they might just sit back and stop trying, before it was certain that the museum wanted to buy it.

114

'I'll give you the gen tomorrow,' said Rory. 'When can I see you?'

'I'm baby-sitting in the morning. But I told Fiona I'd come to your house in the afternoon,' Lucy told him. 'Ailsa's going to give her a perm, so she can't come out.'

'In that case,' said Rory, 'you'll find me in my room – out of the way of clucking females and the smell of rotten eggs.'

He handed her the chessman as the bell sounded for the start of afternoon school. 'You take care of that, now,' he said hastily, as a bunch of kids came tearing along the corridor. 'And don't tell our Fiona about it.'

Lucy didn't resent Rory's telling her what to do. She knew he wasn't being bossy. He just wanted to do his best for her. She reckoned she would go far before she found a better friend.

3A's last lesson that afternoon was in the language lab. At the end of it Fiona and Hazel rushed off to the playing-field to watch the First Eleven football team practising. Lucy was coming downstairs on her own, some way behind the rest of the class, when she happened to glance out of the big window on the landing. What she saw made her heart skip a beat.

The bearded man was there again, standing on the other side of Torridon Road. She could see him anxiously scanning the faces of the pupils who were beginning to trickle out through the gates, and she didn't need her Celtic sixth sense to tell her he was looking for her.

At the same time it dawned on her why the man was after her. Of course! It was the chessman he wanted. He must be one of the people

Old Hamish had said were dying to get their hands on it. He must have read the report of Old Hamish's accident in *The Graphic* and found out what hospital he was in. Yes! It was obvious. The man had clearly known Old Hamish in the past. He knew he had the chessman. And he had been hovering at the ward door like a vulture until Old Hamish had given Lucy his key. He had probably heard Old Hamish asking her to bring the chessman to the hospital.

She stood at the window, gazing out, her heart banging against her ribs. The trouble was, she couldn't prove anything. This strange man had never even spoken to her. If she told Rory about him (and Rory was the only one she could tell since she was keeping the chessman a secret), he would probably think it was all in her imagination. Men were like that. David was always accusing Mum of having too much imagination.

She squared her shoulders. She was on her own. And somehow she had to give the bearded man the slip. She thought she knew how she could do it, too. She ran down the stairs to the cloakroom, grabbed her coat, then raced the length of a corridor leading to one of the fire exits. Once outside, she made for the shrubbery beyond the boiler-room, wriggled through the bushes, and climbed over the railings into Duich Drive. There was no back gate to the school, so the drive was empty. She started running along to her left. After about five minutes, she came to a footpath between two blocks of houses. She turned down it. Her mouth was dry, her heart racing. The path led to Torridon Road. At the end of it, she stopped and poked her head out cautiously. It was all right. There were still plenty of school-children trailing along, but no sign of the bearded man. She turned to her right and set off at a jog-trot towards Nevis Drive.

Lucy hadn't realized what a state she was in until she walked into the living-room and her mother and David stared at her in astonishment. Then a quick glance in the mirror above the fireplace showed her her perspiring crimson face with her eyes starting out of her head and leaves sticking in her hair.

'Practising for sports-day,' she gasped.

To her relief, neither her mother nor David pursued the matter. They were both too pre-occupied with their preparations for tomorrow. David hurried out to clean his car. (He and Laura Bell were taking Granny Black, Miss McCracken, and Mrs Burns to the funeral in the morning.) And Lucy's mother went into the kitchenette to begin scrubbing viciously at the stains on Reuben's anorak so that Gran Campbell wouldn't faint with horror when she saw it. Lucy was glad she had opted out of going to visit Gran at Seahills. She had made the excuse of having to work on her poem for the competition.

She stood by her bedroom door for a few minutes watching her mother. Mum's lips were moving as though she were talking to herself. Lucy could guess what she was doing. She was rehearsing what she would say to Gran Campbell tomorrow when she asked her if she could lend them any money.

Poor Mum! She was going to hate every minute of that interview. And if the British Museum did offer a lot of money for Old Hamish's chessman, she was going to be furious when she remembered how she had had to beg from Gran. For a moment Lucy was tempted to rush over and tell her mother the whole story, including her suspicions about the bearded man. But then Reuben came howling in from the garden with a bloody knee. And, in the resultant pandemonium, Lucy's moment of weakness passed.

It was just as well, she decided, as she lay in bed that night trying to get to sleep. She would never have been able to put a rein on her mother's wild optimism.

17

A Late Snowfall

It was a bitterly cold, grey morning. Just the weather for a funeral, Lucy thought bleakly. She was so tense she could not keep still. She stood up. Sat down. Then stood up again. Although the whole house needed tidying, she couldn't stay still long enough to make a start anywhere. She wandered through all the bedrooms, but keeping well back from the windows, just in case the bearded man was around.

The chilling thought that he must know where she lived (since the report in *The Graphic* had given her address) had shot into Lucy's mind last night, just as she was drifting off to sleep. It had kept her wide awake and worrying for hours. Daylight had chased away most of her panic. She told herself that the man would have turned up at their house before now had he not been afraid of meeting her parents. He was obviously hoping to waylay her when she was on her own, to persuade her to part with the chessman. He certainly looked more of a confidence trickster than a villain. Still, it was best to be on the safe side and stay watchful . . .

Lucy wandered disconsolately out of Reuben's bedroom and back into the living-room. She had allowed Reuben to go out to play in the back garden. She hoped it wasn't too cold for him. She watched him for a few minutes, racing between the two clothes-poles, playing tag with Rufus. He certainly looked warm enough, his cheeks as red as holly berries.

The mantelpiece clock chimed dolefully. Lucy sighed. Was it really only ten o'clock? They would just be halfway through the funeral. Thank goodness Mum had asked her to stay at home with Reuben! She had never been to a funeral, and wasn't looking forward to the experience.

The living-room door flew open and Reuben came stamping in. He tore his coat off and threw it on the floor. Then he ran across to the piano, lifted the lid, put his foot on the loud pedal, and brought his fists down on the keys. Crash! Crash! Crash!

'Stop that!' yelled Lucy, sticking her fingers in her ears.

Reuben whirled round and glared at her indignantly. 'It's my funeral-march!' he cried.

Lucy drew her breath in sharply. Reuben had not been told about Old Hamish's death. David had wanted to tell him, but Mum had said that he was too young. She had gone red-faced and staring-eyed about it. So in the end David had agreed that they would pretend Old Hamish was still in hospital and that, after a while, they would tell Reuben the old man had moved to another house. But had Reuben been listening to people talking? Did he know the truth?

'Whose funeral are you playing the march for?' she asked sharply.

'Paraffin's. He was Rufus's friend,' said Reuben, gazing dreamily out of the window. 'We've just buried him in the rhubarb. He was a cat from a hot country, and he came

120

to Scotland and died of drink and bronichal trouble.'

After a moment he gave Lucy a lopsided grin and turned back to the piano.

'De-ad! De-ad! De-ad!' he wailed.

Crash! Crash! Crash! went the keys.

He's heard Granny Black talking, Lucy thought shrewdly. She always says 'bronichal'. I bet he knows Old Hamish is dead. He's been kidding us all along. The sly wee devil!

Crash! Crash! Crash!

Lucy strode across the room and hauled Reuben from the piano so roughly that he fell over. He opened his mouth and began to bawl. He hadn't really hurt himself, but he might easily have done so.

Lucy felt ashamed of herself. What was wrong with her, pulling a little kid about like that? She ran into the kitchenette and found a chocolate-wafer biscuit for him, the last one in the tin. After wiping his tears away with a tissue she gave him the biscuit.

'Ta,' he said, with a little sob. Then he gave her a watery grin. Lucy nearly burst out crying in remorse.

She walked into her room and stared out at the grey sky. She was becoming a nervous wreck. Too much had happened to her recently. In the past few weeks she had never stopped worrying: about David and the insurance money; about Mum's extravagance; about the poem she had to write for the competition; about Old Hamish; about the bearded man. It was too much for her to cope with.

Then that familiar, steadying hand seemed to fall on her shoulder again. A voice in her head pointed out that if she sold the chessman to the

British Museum most of her problems would be solved. David's debt could be paid off. Mum would calm down. The man would go away. She would only have her poem to worry about.

'De-ad! De-ad! De-ad!' sounded hollowly in the living-room.

Crash! Crash! Crash! went the piano keys. But this time Lucy's nerves didn't jangle in response. She was in control of herself again, thanks to Marmion Bell.

'Lucy!' cried Fiona from under the dryer. 'It's *snowing!*'

Lucy turned to look out of the window and grinned happily. She gave Fiona a thumbs-up sign. She loved snow. Life was wonderful.

Fifteen minutes ago, while Ailsa was neutralizing Fiona's permed curls in the kitchen, Lucy had slipped upstairs to see Rory, who had given her a piece of paper with the address of the British Museum on it, as well as the name of the curator she would have to contact about her chessman. Rory said Lucy should send the chessman to the museum by registered post. She was going to do so at lunch-time on Monday.

The Donalds' telephone, which sat on a small table by the fireplace, suddenly started to ring. Ailsa, feeding towels into the washing-machine in the kitchen, couldn't hear it. Fiona signalled to Lucy to answer it. When she did, she heard her mother's voice asking to speak to her.

'This *is* me,' Lucy cried.

'Oh, good,' said her mother dully. 'Listen, pet. There's a proper blizzard blowing here. There's no way we can leave – particularly when we have Reuben with us. I think we might have to stay the night. Will you be all right on your own?'

'Yes. Of course,' said Lucy cheerfully. She felt that nothing could daunt her today.

'If we do decide to start for home this evening, we'll ring you,' said her mother. 'Otherwise we'll see you in the morning.'

Lucy could tell from Mum's flat, dispirited voice that the trip had not been a success and that Gran had not lent them the money. If only she could have told her about the chessman! If only she could say, 'Stop worrying, Mum. I think our problem's solved.' But she couldn't. Not until she knew for certain.

'Why not stay here for the night? Mum won't mind,' Ailsa said when Lucy had explained why her mother had telephoned.

'Thanks,' said Lucy. 'But I'd better go home. I'll have to light the fire, or we'll have no hot water. Anyway, I must work on my poem. I promised myself I would.'

Her spirits fell a little at the thought of another evening 'struggling with the Muse' as the Head jocularly put it.

Little did Mr Ross know that she felt like throttling the Muse by now, as well as Aggie who had landed her in this predicament. She was equally annoyed with The Great Douglas, who made Lucy feel like a pathetic non-starter, each time they 'conferred'. Occasionally – when she was feeling really down – she even began to harbour a grudge against Marmion Bell. After all, she would tell herself, he had come to her aid on the afternoon of Old Hamish's accident readily enough. Why couldn't he help her to write a poem?

By five o'clock the snow had stopped. But it was deep enough to cover the tops of Mrs Donald's court-shoes as she and Mr Donald walked home from the bus-stop. Mrs Donald was holding her chilled, blue feet against the hall radiator, as Rory left for his badminton club.

The smell of Ailsa's perm-lotion still hung heavy in the air. Rory looked down meaningly at his mother's feet and wrinkled his nose. 'Why not try one of those foot deodorants, Mum?' he said as he slipped past her.

'Rory!' Mrs Donald squealed, aiming a swipe at his head.

'Rude pig!' Fiona yelled after him, as the front door closed. Rory had almost split his sides when he had seen her new hairdo. She wasn't going to forgive him in a hurry.

'At least we'll have our tea in peace, with him out of the way,' Ailsa observed with a sniff.

'Yes. Thank heavens for small mercies,' said Fiona.

Lucy didn't thank heaven at all. She found tea-time at the Donalds' deadly dull without Rory. She really missed him.

18

A Line of Footprints

Lucy left the Donalds' at eight o'clock, later than she had planned. It was bright moonlight. The snow, which was lying a couple of inches deep, seeped through her cheap trainers. But she didn't care. She had the chessman in her pocket, and with it was the paper with the curator's name and the museum's address on it. The future was looking brighter than it had done for weeks. What did a trifle like wet feet matter? She could dry them easily enough when she got home.

It was winter sports time in Bunnyland. The kids were all rushing about laughing and screaming, building snowmen in their gardens, and snowballing each other beneath the street-lamps. Fathers and mothers were out, too, playing with toddlers, even pulling them along on toboggans. This was the first snowfall at the end of a mild winter, and it would probably be the last, so they were obviously determined to enjoy it.

By contrast, on the other side of Whitefields Road, it was like the grave. Most of the residents there were elderly, and, when it snowed, they automatically pulled their curtains, locked their doors, and built up their fires. Lucy was the first to walk along the pavement on the right-hand side of Nevis Drive. She looked back at her line of footprints now marring the perfect whiteness, and a possible first line for a poem floated into her head.

Gently the moon's silver light falls on a line of footprints.

That didn't sound too bad, she decided. Quite promising in fact. But was it too long? Should she finish the first line at 'light'?

Gently the moon's silver light
Falls on a line of footprints.

She had reached her gate and was staring at the path. That was odd: someone had walked up the path over the snow. Someone who had come down Nevis Drive from Torridon Road. It had been a man, by the size of the prints.

Lucy's heart gave a lurch. She had realized the significance of that single line of prints. Whoever had walked along the path to the house hadn't come back. That meant he must still be . . .

A figure suddenly moved out from the shadow at the side of the building. Lucy froze, her hand on the gate. For a horrendous moment she thought – really believed – that Old Hamish had come back to haunt her. Then she heard a familiar dry cough and saw who the small man was who was walking towards her: the bearded man.

Panic washed over her in an icy wave that made her gasp and choke. She turned and began to stumble up Nevis Drive. She thought she heard the man call, 'Hold on a minute!' But there was such a drumming in her ears, she couldn't be sure. She was trying to will strength into her shaking legs, to suck air into her lungs. All that she could think of was that she had the chessman in her pocket and the man was after it. She had to get away.

Her legs gradually gained strength. Soon she

was running quite fast in spite of the snow. Once or twice she slipped but quickly regained her balance. She turned into Torridon Road with no clear idea in her head as to where she was going. An empty bus swooshed by at top speed, throwing up slush. There wasn't a soul in sight. The snow lay like a shroud over the silent gardens and hedges.

A quick glance over her shoulder told her the man was still holding his ground. She ran on, but her pace was slowing. She tried to make her legs go faster only the muscles wouldn't respond. And now the cold air felt like knives in her throat. Her head was beginning to swim. She couldn't keep on. She couldn't! She tottered forward for a few steps. Then suddenly she saw the tall, skeletal shapes of the half-built flats on her right. Scaffolding! she thought. Ladders. Like a hunted animal spying a bolt-hole, she dredged up enough energy to go pelting across the building-site.

'Stop!' the bearded man yelled hoarsely behind her.

But that was the last thing Lucy was going to do, even though the blood was singing in her ears. Once she stumbled on the rough, snow-covered ground and fell headlong. But she picked herself up and staggered on. She could see a ladder.

She was gripping the ladder. She was climbing up it, gasping for breath, whimpering every time her hand or foot slipped from a rung. A kind of plan was beginning to take shape in her brain. If she could get on to the platform she could see above her head, she could knock the man off the ladder. She could kick out at him with her feet, bash him with pieces of wood.

But just as she reached the platform, her strength went quite suddenly, as though someone had pulled out a plug. She groaned, then collapsed in a heap.

'For God's sake, girl! Are you trying to kill yourself?' The man had made no attempt to climb the ladder after Lucy. He was standing by the foot of it, sounding more irritated than angry, more weary than menacing.

Lucy sat up cautiously and stared down at him. His face was lifted up towards her, his features etched clearly in the moonlight. Suddenly she had the disturbing sensation that the man wasn't a stranger to her after all, that she had known him for years. She shivered, feeling herself drifting away from reality, not knowing for a few terrifying seconds if she were awake or in a dream.

Then she suddenly became aware of a painful cramp in her right leg. Her fingers were aching with cold through the wet wool of her gloves. She was awake, all right, and she must do something quickly – something clever. Holding on to a scaffolding pole, she hauled herself slowly to her feet.

'Listen!' she called down shakily to the man below. 'If you're after the chessman, you're too late. I've posted it off to the British Museum. Old Hamish said I was to have it if he died, you know. So I can do what I like with it.'

'I haven't a clue what you're talking about, hen,' the bearded man shouted crossly. Pulling a packet of cigarettes from his overcoat pocket, he lit one with a lighter. Lucy could see his hands shaking. He looked pretty fraught. Then he had a fit of coughing and had to lean against the ladder to catch his breath.

Lucy's courage flooded back. The man, at close quarters, certainly wasn't the type to strike terror into the heart.

'Who are you, anyway?' she called boldly, peering down at him. 'Why do you keep following me? What do you want?'

There was silence for a moment. The man was staring up at her.

'I'm Jimmy Scally,' he said at last. He spoke slowly and distinctly as though he thought Lucy were hard of hearing.

After that they both seemed to be waiting. Lucy for the man to explain himself, the man for some sort of reaction from her. When none came, he pulled up his coat collar and called petulantly, 'Do you not understand what I'm telling you, hen? I'm Jimmy Scally. I'm your father!'

19

The Bearded Man

The man was insane: that was what Lucy thought. He must be sick, too. Perhaps he had had a daughter of Lucy's age who had died. And now his poor brain was imagining that Lucy was she. She would have to be kind to him. But she would have to make him see his mistake.

Still gripping the pole, Lucy leaned forward and looked down earnestly into the bearded man's face. 'No,' she said firmly. 'You're not my father, Mr Scally. My father died fourteen years ago. You've made a mistake. You had better go home.'

But she might have known she wouldn't get rid of him as easily as that, that he wouldn't just nod meekly and go away. He stood motionless for a moment, shocked-looking. Then his face seemed to crumple. Lucy thought he was going to cry. But it wasn't grief that had overwhelmed him. It was exasperation.

'Hell's bells!' he burst out, throwing down his half-smoked cigarette which sizzled and died in the snow. 'So that's what she's told you! I might have guessed. She always managed to complicate things. So now where do I start?'

He turned sideways to Lucy, hands stuffed into his pockets, his shoulders hunched. His face was a sharp silhouette in the moonlight. Suddenly

Lucy found herself staring at his nose. Now she knew why, earlier, the man had seemed familiar. That nose was identical to the one she saw whenever she looked in a mirror. She always thought it was shaped as if someone had chopped it off short.

A wave of giddiness hit her, and she had to grip the pole with two hands to keep herself from falling. She felt as though she were in the dentist's chair, coming out of gas, at that horrible mid-way stage between waking and dreaming. She broke out into a cold sweat.

Without knowing exactly what she was doing, but instinctively seeking the safety of the ground, she backed up to the ladder, found the top rung with one foot and began to climb shakily down.

'Look,' she began weakly when she reached the bottom. All her strength had gone. She felt faint and on the verge of hysterical tears.

But Jimmy Scally wasn't paying attention. He had pulled a wallet from his inside pocket and was searching through it. Suddenly he drew out a black-and-white photograph and held it up, close to Lucy's face.

'Here! Can you see it?' he asked eagerly. 'It's a snap of me and your mother with you, after your christening. Outside Gran Campbell's house. I didn't have a beard in those days, of course.'

The moonlight wasn't strong enough for Lucy to make out the details on the photograph. But she didn't need to. She knew that Jimmy Scally was telling her the truth. Her mother had two photographs taken on the identical spot on the day of Lucy's christening. They must have come from the same spool. One was of Mum and Lucy. The other of Lucy in the arms of Gran. Mum had told her that Marmion Bell had taken them.

A terrible pain was growing inside Lucy's chest. For a wild moment she wondered if she was going to have a heart attack. Then she realized it was just an enormous sob struggling to break out. She moaned and covered her face with her hands. Her brain was spinning.

'Hell!' Jimmy Scally muttered. Lucy heard him light another cigarette. Then his hand touched her shoulder. 'Look, the last thing I wanted to do was upset you like this,' he said contritely. 'But I was desperate, Lucy. I've been trying to run your mother to earth for years. I want a divorce. But I want everything settled up fair and square. And I can't get near the woman! Just when I think I've found her, she vanishes again. I couldn't believe my luck when I saw that picture of you in the paper. Lucy Ashton Bell. (She took the name of Bell, so I wouldn't be able to trace her. I'd to pay a private detective to find that out for me.) I decided to get to you first this time: to send a message to her through you. I had no idea you thought I was dead.'

Lucy broke into a storm of noisy weeping that had been threatening ever since she stepped off the ladder.

Jimmy Scally groaned. 'Come on, hen,' he said wearily, 'let's go back to your house. This is a helluva place to be having a reunion after fourteen years. Will your mother be home by now?'

Lucy shook her head.

'Is she coming home later?'

'They're stuck at Seahills. The snow . . .' Lucy said thickly.

'Well, maybe that's just as well,' her father said. 'I can talk to you first. And you can pave the way for further negotiations, as they say. That's what I hoped for anyway.' He put his hand gently under her elbow and steered her across the rough, snow-covered ground towards the road.

Lucy sat shivering in an armchair while Jimmy Scally lit the fire. She was looking at his hands. He had short, stubby fingers exactly like hers. He moved quickly and deftly. When he had taken his overcoat off, she had seen how neat and tidy he was. She had noticed, too, how he had looked around the messy living-room in disgust when he came in.

As soon as the fire was well alight he went through to the kitchenette and made a pot of tea. Lucy didn't need to tell him where anything was. He found the tea and sugar and milk and even a few digestive biscuits. She could tell her father was a practical man just to look at him. On the way back from the flats he had told her he was a builder. And she could see now, that though he was small and thin, he was wiry and very strong. He talked all the time. He told Lucy how he had been having his morning tea-break when he had seen her photograph in *The Graphic*, and how excited he had felt.

'Lucy Ashton. I knew it must be you,' he said. 'It was your mother who insisted on calling you that. I thought it was a daft name. There was an old Clyde steamer called that, you know.'

Lucy sat gripping her mug of tea with both hands. She neither moved nor spoke.

Jimmy sat down facing her. 'I don't know what your mother's told you about me,' he said, watching her uneasily, 'apart from that lie about me being dead, I mean. I know I behaved badly to her. But there were faults on both sides. It wasn't exactly fun to come home after a hard day's work to find the dinner not cooked and a dirty, untidy house, while she banged away on the piano, the baby howling its head off. Not much fun at all!' His eyes became cold and angry.

'Mind you, I wanted her back,' he went on after a moment. 'I wanted you both back after she ran off with you. I spent months looking for you both. But I'm glad now I never found you. I was young and hot-tempered. I'd probably have murdered her.'

Lucy closed her eyes. She felt as though every word her father spoke was being branded on her brain.

'Are you not going to drink your tea? It'll heat you up,' Jimmy said gently.

She gulped down the hot sweet liquid. But it didn't make her feel any better.

'Och well, it's all water under the bridge,' said Jimmy with a sigh. 'What is important to me now is that I do right by you and your mother. I sold the house last year – the one we bought in Croftpark when we were first married. Half that money's your mother's. There's ten thousand pounds waiting for her in the bank. She'll have a fit when she hears. We bought the house for a fraction of that. I want a divorce as soon as possible. But I want this business of the money settled. Then I can marry my girlfriend and we can emigrate to Australia with a clear conscience.'

Lucy nodded. She felt weak and terribly tired.

'I'll have to be getting home now,' said Jimmy. 'I'm in a rented flat over in Partick at the moment.' He lifted his coat from the back of a chair where he had left it, and pulled a long white envelope from the pocket. 'This letter is for your mother,' he told Lucy. 'I'll put it on the piano here. On the music stand. Will you make sure that she reads it, hen?'

'Yes,' said Lucy dully.

Her father stood looking down at her for a moment. 'This man your mother lives with . . . He treats you well enough?' he asked abruptly.

'Yes,' said Lucy.

'That's all right, then.' He pulled his wallet from his pocket, drew out a sheaf of notes and walked over to shove them in Lucy's hand. 'Buy yourself a present,' he said huskily.

'Thank you,' Lucy said mechanically.

He paused for a moment at the living-room door. 'I'm sorry things didn't work out between your mother and me, hen,' he said tightly. 'You've grown into a fine lassie. I think you've a look of your old man, too.'

Lucy said nothing.

'Goodbye, then,' her father called.

'Goodbye.'

The front door slammed shut. For several minutes Lucy sat like a stone. Then she stared down at her hand as though she'd only just realized she was holding something. Five-pound notes. Ten of them. That was fifty pounds. Her father had given her fifty pounds. Her father!

Suddenly she slipped off the chair on to the rug, her body convulsed by terrible, racking sobs. The cushion tumbled down after her, and she grabbed it and hugged it, trying to draw comfort from it. She began to cry. Noisily at first like a small child. Then with a soft and hopeless keening sound, like someone weeping for the dead. She cried on and on, until there was a band of pain across her chest and her head was pounding. But the real pain was inside her. And she didn't know how she was going to bear it.

20

'Lies, Lies, Lies!'

When Lucy woke, she didn't remember where she was. She couldn't understand why she was so cold, and why her mattress felt so hard. Then she saw the glowing embers of the fire on a level with her face. She sat up stiffly, blinking in the harsh glare of the electric light. It was a moment or two before her eyes focused on the mantelpiece clock. Six o'clock. She rose unsteadily to her feet and looked across at the piano. Yes. Jimmy Scally's letter was propped up on the music stand. She hadn't been dreaming.

It was as though a pain-killing injection had suddenly worn off. The hurt and the shock that had beaten her into the ground last night came back now with renewed force. She staggered around the room, bumping into the furniture, shaking her head, still distraught.

'How could Mum do this to me? How could she do it?' she asked herself.

At the same time, a logical voice inside her head was pointing out that what her mother had done was completely in character. She had invented Marmion Bell – poet, hero, devoted husband and father – because she couldn't face up to the reality of Jimmy Scally and a failed

136

marriage, just as she couldn't face up to the bills that she shoved to the back of the bureau. Only in this case it was Lucy who had had to pay the price of her mother's fantasizing.

Lucy felt that she didn't know who she was any more. That was the worst part. If there had never been a Marmion Bell, there was no Lucy Bell. There was no poet-father. No talent to inherit. It was as though her past had suddenly vanished behind the mist of her mother's lies.

'Lies! Lies! Lies!' Her own voice was ringing in her ears. She had shouted the words aloud. Perhaps she was going out of her mind . . .

She began to cry again, hot tears gushing out of her eyes as though they would never stop. She leaned against the piano, cushioning her head on her arm. She hated her mother. Really hated her for having done this to her. She was going to get back at her. She was going to make her suffer. Rage boiled up inside her, making her shake as though she had a fever.

She rubbed the tears from her cheek with her cuff. Then she realized she was clutching something in her right hand. It was the sheaf of five-pound notes her father had given her. She had forgotten all about them. Never before had she had so much money.

As she stared down at it, she suddenly knew what she could do to take revenge on her mother. She would run away from home. When her mother, David and Reuben arrived back from Seahills, she would be gone. Mum would find Jimmy Scally's letter, and Lucy would be gone. She would go frantic. Good! It was what she deserved. She had obviously been a hopeless wife. Well, as far as Lucy was concerned, she was a hopeless mother. She didn't care if she never saw her again.

It was daylight by now. Lucy switched off the light and pulled back the curtains. It was a wet, grey, depressing morning. There wasn't a trace left of last night's snow. She went to the bathroom and splashed cold water over her face and hands to see if it would make her brain less muzzy. Even after she had washed it, her face still looked ghastly: swollen and blotchy from weeping. She didn't care. She didn't even bother to comb her hair.

She made herself a cup of strong coffee and a slice of toast. She couldn't eat the toast, though. Even the smallest piece stuck in her throat. Her brain felt numb. She must decide where she was going. But she couldn't think of anywhere. She had laid her money on the living-room table. She decided she ought to put it in her purse. Her duffel coat, still damp, was lying across the sofa where she had thrown it last night. She walked over and plunged her hand into the wrong pocket, the right-hand one. Her fingers gripped not her purse, but Old Hamish's chessman.

The chessman! It was as though a fuse in her brain had suddenly been mended. She came to life. She knew where she was going to head for. London! She would take the chessman to the museum, then live rough until the money came through. Hundreds of kids lived rough in London. She had seen programmes about them on television. Then, she had felt horrified by what she had seen. But now she was prepared to be one of the rootless ones too. If she took her quilt, a few changes of underclothes and a couple of warm sweaters, she would survive for a few weeks. The worst of the winter was over. Anyway, the weather was much milder in London than it was in Glasgow. And once she had the money for the chessman . . . But she couldn't think that far ahead. Her brain wasn't up to it. What she had to decide now was how she would get to London.

There was an old army kitbag hanging in the living-room cupboard. Lucy took it into her bedroom. She was shaking with excitement. She stuffed her quilt into her bag, then managed to shove in three pairs of knickers, a tee-shirt, a sweater and a towel. She slipped in an unopened bar of soap before pulling the bag's drawstring tight. Then she hoisted it experimentally on to her shoulder. It wasn't too heavy. She would manage as long as she didn't have to walk any distance. Once she was in London, she could leave it in a left-luggage locker during the day.

The thought of walking round London on her own sent an icy shiver down her spine. She had never been to London – not even with a school-party. She was fourteen years old, and she had never been to London. Dear old Mum, always short of money, had seen to that. Lucy's lips tightened into a hard, resentful line.

She went into the lobby and looked up the number of the coach station in the telephone directory. When she got through, she found herself listening to a talking-timetable. It said there was a coach leaving for London at nine a.m. She put down the receiver. That was all she needed to know. She would catch that coach. But from what she could remember, the first local bus didn't leave Whitefields terminus until half past nine on Sundays. So she would have to order a taxi. She looked up the Yellow Pages and found a twenty-four-hour taxi-service. She ordered a cab for eight. She was going to lay a false trail. She would ask the driver to take her to Queen Street railway station. Then she would walk from there to the coach station. It wasn't far.

What was the age limit for half-fare travel on a coach? she wondered. She would have to risk asking for it anyway. She must keep as much money as possible so as to be able to live on her own in London. But she shouldn't have any problems. She was small and on the thin side. Strangers always thought she was younger than she was.

She made some cheese sandwiches and shoved them into her coat pocket beside the chessman. Then she put the money into her purse and pushed it into the other pocket. It was only half past seven. She had half an hour before the taxi arrived. She wandered into her room and looked around her for what was probably the last time. This was where she had written her 'hero' essay – a load of lies, had she only known it. No wonder her mother had nearly had a fit when she had seen all her fairytales recounted so naively by Lucy. And no wonder I can't write poetry, Lucy thought bitterly. Now, maybe if they had asked me to lay a few bricks . . .

Her throat suddenly felt as though it were full of broken glass. She was on the verge of tears again. She must take a grip on herself. If she went to the coach station looking as though she had been weeping she would only attract attention. People would think she was a kid running away from home after a row with her parents. Whereas she wanted to look like a girl going off on holiday to her aunt's in London. That was the story she was prepared to tell if anyone challenged her. She picked up her comb from her dressing-table and ran it through her hair, before slipping it into the back pocket of her jeans. Then she bathed her eyes again while she waited for the taxi to arrive.

21

Running Away

Lucy arrived at the coach station at twenty minutes to nine. To begin with she could find no one who could tell her from which bay the London coach left. When she finally tracked it down, she discovered why. It was a brand-new service, starting that morning.

The driver was leaning against the door talking to a mate. Lucy could hear him saying that the coach picked passengers up in Kirktown, Cumnock, and Dumfries and wasn't due in at Victoria until ten p.m. That was probably an advantage, she decided. There was bound to be a waiting-room in a coach station like Victoria. She would just stay there until Monday morning, when she could begin exploring London.

The ticket office was closed, so the few people who were boarding the coach without tickets had to buy them from the driver. Lucy took a deep breath and walked towards him. What if he challenged her about the half-fare? Or started asking awkward questions about her travelling on her own? But before she reached him, she was pushed aside by a crowd of noisy punks obviously returning from an all-night party. They were boys, some with shaven heads, others with multi-coloured cockscombs. They were all brandishing tickets which they shoved laughingly under the driver's nose. He nodded glumly and stood aside to let them board the coach, and was still staring worriedly after them when Lucy asked for her half-fare single ticket. He hardly glanced at her as he gave her her ticket and change. She was congratulating herself on this auspicious start when she suddenly began to see stars.

The stars were passing in a continuous procession, from left to right, in front of her eyes. A particularly bright one went sailing by as she slipped into an empty double seat near the back of the coach. At the same time she felt her fingers beginning to tingle, and she broke out into a cold sweat.

Probably Lucy's panicking accelerated matters. At any rate, by the time the coach pulled out of the station, the tingling in her fingers had crept halfway up her arms, and the stars had been joined by dazzling, zig-zagging lights. She was sure now that she was having one of her rare attacks of migraine. The question was, could she cope with it on such a long journey?

Lucy had had enough migraine attacks to be familiar with the pattern they invariably took. She would probably see flashing lights and stars for another fifteen minutes or so. The funny, tingling feeling would creep further and further up her arms and might even affect her face. Then the terrible blinding headache would start and she would feel deathly sick. If the attack were really severe, she would end up vomiting and with diarrhoea, too. What on earth was she going to do if that happened? There wasn't even a loo on the coach.

She closed her eyes as the coach rattled

through the quiet southern suburbs. But it was no good. She couldn't shut out the flashing lights and the stars. Behind her the punks were already growing rowdy. One of them had obviously been home to celebrate his twenty-first birthday and had brought some London mates up with him.

'Twenty-one yester-*die*!' they yelled in chorus as they banged him on the back.

There was a clink of bottles. The driver turned to glare at them.

It was nine thirty and raining hard when they drew into Kirktown coach station. For the past ten minutes Lucy's head had felt as though it were being gripped in a giant vice. Nausea was rolling over her in continuous waves. She was shivering with cold.

The driver had twice stopped the coach on the moors and gone along to the rear of it to stop the punks stamping and singing. Now he got out and disappeared at a run round the side of a building. A group of new passengers hovered uncertainly by the coach's open door, wondering whether they could get on without showing their tickets. Two of the punks thudded along the passageway grinning at everyone. One of them shouted that he was going to have a pee.

'We're going for two pees!' his mate screamed, laughing hysterically.

Lucy's head felt as though it were going to explode. She thought she would get out and see if the fresh air would help her. Glancing at the punks over her shoulder, she decided it would be safer to take her bag with her. It was just as well she did. As soon as the cold, damp air hit her, she turned violently giddy, and her stomach began to heave. She walked a few paces and leaned back against a wall for support, staring bleakly at the London coach. The idea of being shut inside it for another twelve and a half hours was unbearable. She just couldn't face it. London was out. She felt so ill, she didn't even care that she had thrown away her fare. All she wanted to do was lie down in a quiet room with the curtains closed.

As though in answer to her prayer, a bus began to creep out of a garage just across from where she was standing. Its indicator-board said 'Seahills'. A sleepy-looking conductress was walking towards it. Lucy knew that Gran Campbell often came to Kirktown to do her shopping, and that it was only a fifteen minutes' ride here to Seahills. She gave a little sob of relief and started running unsteadily through the puddles to the bus. The conductress climbed on, and Lucy followed, half falling into a seat near the front.

As the bus slid out of the station, Lucy put her hand in her pocket and discovered that her purse was missing. Luckily she had shoved her three pounds change into her other pocket. She was in such a state she didn't care that she had lost all that money. Then when she asked for a single to Seahills, she found her speech was slurred. This had happened to her once before during a really severe migraine attack. The conductress, who was middle-aged with a white, lined face, shook her head in disgust as she handed Lucy her ticket. She obviously thought the girl was drunk or drugged, or suffering from a hangover. Lucy ignored her. Her world had shrunk to a circlet of pain clamped round her head. She couldn't think or feel beyond it.

The fifteen minutes that followed seemed like eternity. Lucy was dimly aware of bleak, empty, rainswept streets, and of houses flashing by.

Then fields and hedges. Then houses again. More fields. More houses. Once she looked over to her right and caught a glimpse of grey sea. At last, just when she thought she couldn't hold out a moment longer but would be sick on the floor, she saw the sign that said 'Seahills Welcomes Careful Drivers'. And there ahead was the spire of the red sandstone church that stood on the corner of Craig Drive where Gran Campbell lived. There was a bus-stop outside the church. Lucy got to her feet and staggered the few steps to the door. The conductress, who had been dozing on the long side-seat, reached up and pinged the bell.

'I'm sorry for mothers nowadays, so I am!' she shouted angrily after Lucy, as the girl jumped down from the bus and staggered across the wet pavement.

Lucy stood blinking. She found herself looking up not at one, but at two spires. Now she was suffering from double-vision. That had never happened to her before. This was the worst migraine attack she had ever had.

Five minutes later she was standing in her grandmother's immaculate porch, her eyes half-closed as she rang the bell. The door opened and Gran's startled face looked out.

'Lucy!' she gasped. 'What's happened? What on earth are you doing . . . '

Before Mrs Campbell could say any more, Lucy was violently sick over the red, polished doorstep.

22

Father's Day

Lucy lay on top of the bed in her grandmother's spare room with the quilt over her. The curtains were closed and a handkerchief, soaked in eau-de-cologne, lay on her brow. Gran had given her two pain-killing tablets and a cup of sweet coffee, and already the pain had receded far enough to allow her to become drowsy.

She had told her grandmother that she had been running away to London – no more. And now Gran was phoning Mum to tell her that Lucy was with her. The telephone was in the hall, and Lucy could hear her grandmother's exclamations of surprise, then the long gaps during which Mum must be telling her about Jimmy Scally's letter. When Gran spoke, it was in a low voice, but from time to time Lucy could hear her own name mentioned. She couldn't work up any interest in what was being said about her, though. She didn't even care that her flight had come to such an ignominious end. All she wanted to do was sleep, and for the pain to be gone when she wakened.

In a little while Gran came back into the room and sat on the edge of Lucy's bed. She took the handkerchief from Lucy's forehead and substituted her own cool hand. It was beautifully soothing. As Lucy looked up at her grandmother, she suddenly realized that she had exactly the same eyes and mouth as Mum. It seemed incredible that she had never noticed this before – that she had seen only a smartly-dressed, elderly woman with white, permed hair. Gran smiled at her but didn't speak. Lucy closed her eyes. Within minutes she was sleeping.

When she woke it was three o'clock in the afternoon and her migraine attack was over. It was what she had prayed for. But with the headache gone, the other pain – the one that couldn't be cured with aspirins – came surging back. She sat up and pulled back the curtains. The rain was beating slantwise across Gran's long, narrow garden. The sky was a low, grey lid. Lucy felt totally without hope.

Gran looked in and smiled at her. 'Head better?'

Lucy nodded.

'I've saved some chicken and some pineapple jelly for you. Do you want to come and eat it now?'

'I'm not hungry,' Lucy said in a flat voice.

'You must eat,' said Gran firmly. 'Otherwise the headache will start up again. Come along, dear. Be sensible.'

Lucy sighed and swung her legs off the bed. She followed her grandmother into the small, shining dining-room where her Yorkshire cousins, Selina and Amanda, smiled haughtily from a new silver-framed photograph on top of the sideboard. Did they know about Jimmy Scally? Lucy wondered.

'Sit down, pet,' said Gran brightly, nodding towards the place she had set for Lucy at the table. 'Eat up. I'll go and make some coffee.'

Once she had tasted the chicken Lucy found

she was ravenous. After all, she hadn't eaten properly since last night. By the time her grandmother brought the coffee, she had finished both the chicken and the jelly.

Then all at once she noticed what Gran had been doing while she waited for Lucy to wake up. A pile of old photographs was spilling out of a large brown envelope on to the green velvet settee. Amongst them Lucy could see another print of the photograph that Jimmy Scally had shown her last night. Immediately she was seething again, and shaking with anger. Her mother had behaved abominably towards her. But so had Gran. She had stood by for years watching Lucy being fed lies. It was disgusting.

'I'll never forgive any of you for what has happened to me,' she burst out savagely. 'Have you any idea what it feels like, Gran, to discover that the man you thought was your father never even existed? And that your true father's not dead at all? Can you imagine it?'

'Well, don't blame me for that, Lucy,' said her grandmother, glaring at her. 'I always said your mother's idea was absolutely crazy. I told her so from the start.'

'My mother!' said Lucy with a sneer. 'What a joke! What kind of a mother has she been? A mother's supposed to look after her children – to stop them getting hurt. She . . . she . . . she thinks of no one but herself,' she stammered, holding back her tears.

Gran Campbell stiffened and her chin went up. 'Ah! Now! But that's not fair,' she said sharply. 'No, Lucy. I won't allow you to say that. That is just not true.'

'It *is* true,' wailed Lucy. 'Mum wanted to forget her rotten marriage to Jimmy Scally – to my father. So she invented Marmion Bell. She never spared a thought for what might happen to me.'

'But, Lucy, it was *all* for you,' cried her grandmother, jumping to her feet. Her eyes were starting out of her head, just like Mrs Bell's did when she was in a state. 'It was because of what Scally did to you that your mother left him. That's why she's scurried about the country for fourteen years like a hunted animal. "How can I let my child grow up knowing that her father did that to her?" She's said that to me umpteen times, Lucy. That was why she invented Marmion Bell. Your mother's every kind of fool. But I will not let you say that she doesn't love you.'

Lucy stared at her grandmother. After a moment she said very quietly, 'What was it that my father did to me?'

There was a long silence during which Gran Campbell could be seen to come to a decision.

'All right. It seems to me that you must hear the truth now,' she said at last. 'So, rightly or wrongly, I will take it upon myself to tell you.'

'What?' Lucy's voice was barely audible.

'Jimmy Scally came home one night in a drunken temper, picked you out of your carry-cot, and hurled you against the wall,' her grandmother said crisply.

'What?'

'Yes. You were four months old. It was the middle of winter. The snow was on the ground. Your mother ran two miles with you to the casualty department of the infirmary. Your head was bleeding. You still have the scar above your temple. Luckily there was no serious damage. Laura told them she had fallen downstairs while she was carrying you, and they believed her. She came straight to me that night, all the way from

Glasgow, in a taxi. And the next day she set off on her travels with you. She saw an advert for Bell's whisky from the train and decided that would be your new name. I helped her out with money, and so did your Aunt Rose. Then she found herself work. Scally bothered me for a bit until I complained to the police and they warned him off.'

Lucy closed her eyes. A great pang went through her. She wanted to see her mother. She wanted to hug her, tell her that now she understood about Marmion Bell.

'Mind you, Laura brought it on herself,' Gran Campbell rattled on as she carried the dirty dishes through to the kitchen and started washing up. 'She had a brilliant musical career ahead of her when she met Scally. He was a bricklayer then. It was one of those ridiculous infatuations. They had nothing in common. We all tried to talk her out of it. But she wouldn't listen. That marriage killed your poor grandfather. He was dead within six months of it. And then when she ran away from Scally she was left with nothing. That's probably why she's been in debt ever since. I can hardly believe that Scally wants to give her half the money he got for the house. He must surely have improved with his keeping! Mind you, your mother never learns, does she? This David's turned out to be a dead loss as well . . .'

Lucy decided she didn't want to hear any more. She slipped out into the hall to telephone home and ask David if he could please come soon to collect her.

They drove across the moors in the dusk, the windscreen wipers clicking like a metronome.

Lucy lay resting against the cushions that David had put along the back seat for her, and the poem slipped into her head, line by line.

'I'm your father,' he said.
The small thin man with the cough,
'Come back from the dead to claim you,
Come back to kill your dream of me.'
Blind, deaf, bleeding, Dream Father squirms on the ground,
Real Father lives, come back to claim me,
Dream Father dies without a sound.
Let me follow him. But I cannot follow him.
I must climb down to the ground,
To the small man with the cigarette
In his mouth.
Father!

She said the lines over and over to herself as they sped towards Glasgow. It was the first poem she had ever composed. It was her elegy for Marmion Bell.

23

Free

Lucy's headache had not been a simple migraine. By the time she got home from Seahills, her temperature was high and she had a swollen face.

'It's Scally's fault!' cried Mrs Bell angrily. 'He's made her ill by giving the child such a shock. He's as big a fool as ever he was.'

But when David ran Lucy along to the surgery on Monday morning, the doctor diagnosed a severe attack of sinusitis and prescribed anti-biotics and bed-rest until she felt better.

Lucy had never been much good at playing the invalid. It had always been a job to persuade her to stay in bed when she was ill. But now she was reluctant to leave it, even after the fever and swelling had both gone. Her white face grew thinner and sharper, her eyes larger and perma-nently anxious-looking. Whenever David peeped in at her he found her lying listlessly, hands on top of the cover, staring into space. She made an effort to smile when he tried to cheer her up, but it was an effort. He could see that. So he worried about her.

Mrs Bell worried frantically too. She began to think she had damaged Lucy irreparably by inventing Marmion Bell, though she had done it with the best of intentions. She sat on the edge of

Lucy's bed in the evenings trying to talk her back to normality, telling her how, for years, she had lived in terror of Scally's tracking them down and snatching Lucy back; how, as time passed, Scally became more and more of a monster in her imagination so that, even now, she couldn't bear to meet him, but was making all the arrangements for the divorce through her lawyer.

'Not that he wants to see me,' she added quickly. 'Now that he has salved his conscience, he wants to forget that you and I exist . . . which is all to the good. No one else needs to know he exists, either, Lucy. You're still Lucy Bell.'

Lucy understood all this. But she could not respond, either in words or feelings. It was as though not only her mother, but the rest of the world, had been suddenly cut off from her by an impenetrable sheet of glass. She lay in bed watching them going about their daily activities as though she were looking into a fish tank. It was weird. Horrible. But she could do nothing about it.

Fiona and Hazel came to see her on Thursday, giggling and excited because, at afternoon break, the P.E. teacher had asked them to take a note to the prefects' room for The Great Douglas. Lucy could not even raise a smile.

On Friday afternoon Rory arrived to find out what Lucy had done about the chessman. When she said, in a flat voice, 'Nothing,' he offered to take it away, parcel it up, and post it off, with a note, to the museum. Lucy said, 'All right. If you want to. It's in my coat pocket.' She couldn't have cared less, in fact.

She lay quiet and troubled-looking for another four days, dimly aware that she ought to be feeling thankful for many things. Already, Mr Tomney's thousand pounds had been repaid.

Mum had been able to open a savings-account for the first time in fifteen years, and she and David were making wedding plans. David had applied for a place at university to train as a social worker. Mum said this time he would pass his exams, because his heart would be in his work. Reuben was wild with excitement because Mum had promised to buy him a pup, as soon as David had put a fence round their garden. Everyone was happy, and looking forward to the future . . . except Lucy.

Then, on Wednesday, Rory came back to see her, shoulders drooping, freckles hidden by a shamefaced blush.

'I hardly know how to tell you this,' he said miserably, pulling a small, padded envelope from his pocket and dropping it on the dressing-table. 'The museum sent the chessman back by return of post. Apparently it's just a very clever replica. They've had several sent in over the years. They were made in the 1920s by some joker in Edinburgh. They reckon it's worth about fifteen pounds for its curiosity value. So your old friend, Hamish, was conned, I'm afraid.'

'Just as well he never found out. The air would have been blue with his swearing from here to Loch Lomond,' said Lucy with a faint smile.

'I'm terribly sorry,' said Rory.

'It doesn't matter,' Lucy said truthfully. 'I don't mind at all.'

Rory thought she was being brave. He looked quickly away from her sad, white face and his eye fell on a sheet of paper lying on top of the book cupboard. It was Lucy's poem. She had written it down on the Sunday night when she had come back from Seahills and had given it a title, 'Father's Day'. Rory picked it up.

'Oh, don't,' Lucy murmured in a pained voice. No other eyes had read it.

Rory didn't hear her. He read the poem from beginning to end with great attention. When he looked at Lucy his eyes were glowing.

'I like it,' he said. 'I'm not sure that I understand it. But I like it. It's different. I'm sure it will stand a good chance of winning.'

'But it's not for . . .' Lucy started.

Then she became aware that her heart was racing wildly and that her cheeks were hot, not with embarrassment, but with happiness. Rory's approval of her poem had pierced the glass wall. She was free. It hadn't been enough to write the poem down for herself. A poet had to pull the curtain back and let the world look in. That was the secret of release. That was what Marmion . . .

She gave a tremulous sigh. Then, for the first time in ages, really smiled.

'Thanks, Rory,' she said. 'I suppose it's not bad for a first poem. But it won't be anywhere near as good as Douglas Gordon's entry.'

The first of June. A Monday. Raining. Yet the Head was fairly bouncing across the platform, grinning, delighted about something. What? Not the sports results. The weekend had been a washout: no tennis, no cricket.

'The results of the David Hogg Memorial Poetry Competition,' Mr Ross announced, waving a green sheet of paper in the air. His eyebrows were going up and down like Groucho Marx's, a sure sign of extreme excitement.

The majority of pupils in the hall had either forgotten about the competition, or had never heard of it in the first place. Still, anything to brighten up a wet Monday! There was a general stir of anticipation. Feet shuffled. Eyes brightened expectantly.

'Douglas has won! He's won!' Lucy heard Fiona say in a tremulous voice.

Lucy believed it.

The Great Douglas believed it too. Lucy saw him raise his head and pull back his shoulders a little as though he were bracing himself to receive the applause.

'We have a winner!' cried the Head.

A ripple of excitement ran through the hall. Aggie McLintock was looking at Mr Ross doubtfully, as though she thought he had been watching too many television quiz-games.

'A first prize of one hundred pounds, and five hundred pounds worth of books for the school, has been won by Lucy Bell of 3A for her poem, "Father's Day", which the judges thought "highly original and very moving",' the Head announced jubilantly.

Everyone cheered. 3A went potty in a body, jumping up and down and shrieking. The Great Douglas recovered himself quickly enough to join in the clapping. Aggie stood grinning like a Cheshire cat. Lucy cried.

Ten minutes later as she stood in the corridor, still dazed, showing her admiring classmates her cheque, Rory Donald pushed his way through, swung Lucy off the ground, then kissed her, before hurrying away.

'*Hey!*' Fiona shouted after him. 'What do you think you're *doing*, Rory? I'll tell Dad about this.'

'What's the panic?' said Lucy calmly, turning to stare at her. 'Rory's my friend!'

When Lucy got home, she found David in the living-room reading a book on psychology, and her mother at the piano practising arpeggios. Reuben was in the garden playing with Rufus – the real Rufus – a black-and-white terrier pup. The Housing Company decorators were upstairs in number eight. It was funny to hear sounds up there again. The flat had been rented to a young couple, Jo-Ann Bryce and Andy Thompson, who would soon be moving in. They had come down to introduce themselves on Saturday. Lucy's family had liked them.

Lucy walked slowly across the room and put her hands on her mother's shoulder. Mrs Bell stopped playing.

'I won first prize for my poem,' Lucy said in a shaky voice. 'They've sent me my cheque already. But I've to go and get the medal at a proper ceremony next month.'

'Lucy!' Mrs Bell's large, dark eyes turned shiny with happiness. After a moment a tear rolled down her cheek. 'Oh, Lucy! I'm so proud!' she gasped.

Mrs Bell had had a shock when Lucy had first shown her the poem. She hadn't wanted her to enter it for the competition. But David, soon to be Lucy's stepfather – her real stepfather – had said that people wouldn't know Lucy was describing her own experience. And even if they guessed a bit of the truth, so what! Poetry was what was important inside you. Lucy had loved David for that.

Now he threw down his book and came striding over to clap Lucy on the back.

'Clever girl! Great! Fantastic!' he said, chuckling.

'What is it? What has Lucy done?' Reuben came into the living-room, staggering under the weight of Rufus who had gone to sleep with his head on the little boy's shoulder.

'She's won first prize in an important poetry competition. It's marvellous,' said Mrs Bell. Then she asked anxiously, 'But have you wiped your feet, Reuben? And Rufus's muddy paws?'

'Yes,' said Reuben, laying the pup down tenderly on the new green hearthrug, before giving Lucy a hug.

Lucy put one arm around her little brother, her eyes misty with happiness. The sun had finally broken through the overcast sky and was shining in at the window. It brought out the colours of the new gold and brown carpet and gave a sheen to the creamy wallpaper David had hung last month. The armchairs had been re-covered, and there were pictures on the wall. The living-room was pretty, and tidy, as well as comfortable-looking. Jimmy Scally, who was responsible for its transformation, would not have recognized it now. Best of all, Mum had thought carefully about every penny she had spent on it. Now that she had money in the bank, she wasn't extravagant any more. It was really surprising.

'We'll have to do something,' said David suddenly. 'Have a celebration.'

'The Schumann Piano Concerto on Friday!' cried Mrs Bell, springing to her feet. 'It's that new young pianist we saw on the television. I'll phone now and reserve seats.'

'No. It's to be my treat,' said Lucy, waving her cheque. 'And I'd rather go to the theatre, Mum. They're doing *A Doll's House* at the Citizen's. Aggie says it's fab.'

'Fab?' said her stepfather, raising his eyebrows. 'The Head of English?'

' "First-rate" actually,' admitted Lucy with a grin.

'Right,' said her mother. 'Thank you, darling. We'll enjoy that. Reuben won't though. We'll have to get a sitter for him.'

'Rufus will sit with me, and I'll sit with him. We'll be OK, folks,' Reuben said.

'Rory will come round, if I ask,' said Lucy.

'Oh, yes!' cried Reuben. 'I'll have Rory. He's going to teach me to play chess and make me into a child prodigal.'

Lucy went into her bedroom, threw her bag down on the floor, and picked up her notebook from the book-shelf. She had acquired the habit now of writing a little before tea-time every day. Sometimes she worked on a new poem. On this special day, though, she just wanted to record her feelings.

She sat cross-legged on the floor, sucking the end of her pen. An invisible hand fell on her shoulder, as though giving a blessing. She could feel the warm pressure of the fingers. She could. Really! But how? Then, looking up, she caught sight of Old Hamish's chessman on her dressing-table, no longer malevolent but friendly. Suddenly she felt girdled by love and encouragement and approval.

'Weird! You are turning weird, Lucy Bell,' she warned her reflection.

She grinned. So what? Most writers were pretty peculiar from what she had heard. She closed her eyes and started to shape a sentence in her mind.

THE END